SEVEN MEN RIDING

Sheriff Hab Beely prided himself on having a peaceful town, so he was extremely annoyed when a tough-looking stranger rode in and kicked up a ruckus in Darton's saloon. Hab was getting on in years and he usually let his young deputy, Johnny Carver, handle drunks and suchlike. Trouble was, the stranger was no sooner locked up than a second newcomer put in an appearance, then five others at intervals. Soon, Johnny Carver's natural facility with his six-shooter was about to be put to the test.

Books by Wallace Ford
in the Linford Western Library:

SHOWDOWN IN HIGH VALLEY

WALLACE FORD

SEVEN MEN RIDING

Complete and Unabridged

LINFORD
Leicester

First published in Great Britain in 1995 by
Robert Hale Limited
London

First Linford Edition
published 2001
by arrangement with
Robert Hale Limited
London

British Library CIP Data

Ford, Wallace, *1924* –
    Seven men riding.—Large print ed.—
Linford western library
    1. Large type books 2. Western stories
    I. Title
    823.9'14 [F]

    ISBN 0–7089–9719–8

Published by
F. A. Thorpe (Publishing)
Anstey, Leicestershire

Set by Words & Graphics Ltd.
Anstey, Leicestershire
Printed and bound in Great Britain by
T. J. International Ltd., Padstow, Cornwall

This book is printed on acid-free paper

iding

Neath Port Talbot
Libraries
Llyfrgelloedd
Castell-Nedd
Port Talbot

FORD, W.
....

Seven men riding
....

....

*Books should be returned or renewed by the last date
stamped above.*
*Dylid dychwelyd llyfrau neu eu hadnewyddu erbyn y
dyddiad olaf a nodir uchod*

NP56

1

A stranger had ridden into town and Sheriff Hab Beely didn't care much for the looks of him. It was a quiet hour of the day in Stockwell, many of the stores closing at around one o'clock and opening again at two. It was quiet enough for Hab to hear a horse come single-footing in from the west and presently draw level with him. He gave the lanky, stoop-shouldered rider a casual glance from beneath the brim of his hat. The newcomer saw nothing of this, assuming that the stout man with the badge pinned to his scuffed vest was indulging in *siesta*. The stranger grinned to himself and Hab noticed the way his mouth twisted in a sneer.

Then the newcomer was past. He continued as far as Darton's saloon and brought his bony claybank in at the rack. He dismounted with the manner of someone who had travelled far, crossed to the rail and flipped the claybank's reins to the post. Next, he climbed to the boardwalk and stood there, hat brim cuffed at a go-to-hell angle, hands on lean hips while he peered up and down the length of the street. Again that grin that would make a cat spit, before he wheeled and pushed through the saloon's batwing doors.

Hab Beely had been the sheriff of Morgan County for ten years; for five before that he had been deputy sheriff to old Ezra Blaidsall. But one morning they found Blaidsall dead in bed, which was a right good place to die. Ezra had contracted pneumonia or something of the sort and failed to look after himself properly.

An election had been called and Hab, at forty-five, was presented with Ezra's badge and invested with the full responsibility of running affairs in the county.

Hab had appointed an up and

coming youngster as his deputy, Johnny
Carver, by name. Johnny was the best
horseshoe thrower in the district surrounding Stockwell, the county seat. He
was also a sharp hand at stud poker,
and he could knock an apple from a
fence spike at ten yards with his .45
Colt revolver, drawing and shooting as
fast as any man the citizens of Stockwell
had ever seen in action, all qualifica-
tions which impressed Beely favourably.
So Johnny Carver of the quick draw
and the easy smile was duly sworn in
and given the badge that Hab had
packed for years before him.

It might be said that fifteen years in
the service of law and order could not
fail to leave their mark on a man. Many
a man might have grown sour and
disillusioned with the vagaries of
human nature which he was constantly
called on to contend with. But all Hab
Beely had done was grown a trifle wider
in the midriff and become more
tolerant and mellow in his outlook.

Stockwell was a reasonably peaceful

town in a county that embraced cattle ranches for the most part, a handful of dirt farmers' homesteads, and two or three small sheep outfits that might not have existed for all anyone ever heard of them.

The town had known wilder times. In the 'seventies it had been a railhead jumping-off point, a centre for cattle drives to terminate, and where the woolly cowboys were wont to take the bit in their teeth and get out of hand. Then a new shipping centre had been opened up twenty miles to the south-west, and Stockwell slowly reverted to a more leisurely and peaceful tenor.

These days Hab Beely left the more energetic side of the law work to Johnny Carver. Hab enjoyed sitting in the shade of the law office awning, high-crowned hat tilted over his fore-head, puffing at his pipe, watching the world go past the doorway. He had a friendly greeting for the folks who went to and fro. He knew most of them by sight and addressed them by their first names. When he did happen to spot someone he failed to recognise he made it his business to inquire who he was.

Always at the back of his mind was a notion — perhaps he might admit to it being a fear — that one day something would happen in his bailiwick to disrupt the smooth order of things.

Today, Hab had lunched, as he always did, at Ma Pearson's cafe across the street and two blocks east, and now he was taking it easy with a loaded pipe burning gently between his teeth. He sucked at the stem of his pipe now and frowned. The sun was shining brightly overhead and casting a brittle heat over the brick and frame buildings and the dusty roadway, and yet he was aware of a coldness coming into the region of his spine and settling there. It was an old sensation, an ancient one, and its reawakening was discomfiting, to say the least.

Just then Johnny Carver emerged from Ma Pearson's cafe from having his lunch. The tall young man straightened his hat squarely on his head of straw-coloured hair, brought makings from the pocket of his hickory shirt and built a cigarette. The cigarette burning, he strode into the roadway.

Johnny had a queer awkward grace about him as he walked, like a sailor lately come ashore after a lengthy voyage who had not properly found his land legs. He ambled across the road and put his back against the wall of the office building.

'That Folsom,' he said, sounding as angry as he ever came to being. 'Left the back door of his store open last night. Mutt comes in and rummages around, tears things to hell and yonder. It could have been a robber as well as a dog, I told him. I — Say, Hab, you remind me of a gent that just saw his stepmother stepping off the stage for a month's visit. Anything up?'

'Don't know,' Beely replied slowly. He poked with the stem of his pipe. 'That claybank . . . '

Johnny turned to squint at the racked

6

horse left by the stranger. He whistled. 'Skin and bones, eh? Know whose it is?'

'That's what I mean. I've never seen it before. Nor the fella who was forking it.'

'New neighbour, maybe? Well, we could do with some new faces around this burg. Could do with a bit of livening up, too, I guess.'

'Easy,' Beely rebuked, frowning in spite of the younger man's levity. 'Things could liven the way we don't want 'em. I don't care for the looks of that pilgrim. He's got the sort of face you find on dodgers. Go have a look-see for yourself.'

'He in Darton's?'

The sheriff nodded and Johnny left him. He paused at the front of the saloon, then went over to the claybank at the rail. It nickered from fond memories of other days as he searched through the mane for a neck brand. He found none.

'You could do with a bait of oats, boy. A combing. Ages since I've seen so many burrs in town, all at the one time.'

He swung to the faded batwing doors and breasted them. The saloon trade at this time of day was at a low ebb. Ed Kirby, the bartender, was cleaning glasses and wiping bottles in a desultory fashion. The stranger mentioned by Hab had gone to a table by the wall opposite the counter and had a bottle and glass in front of him. He was lifting the glass to his mouth, savouring the sharp bite of rye whisky. He drank it off quickly and immediately poured again. He appeared to be preoccupied and paid no heed to the blond-haired man with the deputy's badge pinned to his shirt.

'Howdy, Johnny,' Kirby greeted with a broad smile. 'You haven't took to drinking in the middle of the day?'

'Why not? It's a right good time to drink a beer.' Johnny glanced across at the stranger's table and the bartender nodded his understanding.

'Like a gent who's been talking with the devil and lost the argument. See him throw that stuff back?'

'He paying all right?'

'I reckon. It's just that — '

Whatever else Ed Kirby might have said was cut short by the newcomer calling him. 'Hey, barkeep!'

'I hear you. What do you want?'

'Bring me a beer, will you. You got cold beer, I hope?'

'Cool as you'll get it anywhere in this heat.' And in an aside to Johnny Carver: 'Hark at him. Figures we got an ice-house.'

'Hurry it up, mister, will you?'

Kirby fetched the beer and had a dollar spun out to him. 'Bring me my change. No, wait . . . you got cigars?'

'Five cents or — '

'Where's the difference? A smoke's a smoke, ain't it?'

The bartender supplied him with a handful of cigars. Johnny kept his back to the man but observed him in the big mirror while he drank his beer. The stranger sniffed a cigar, scowling all the while. He scratched a match alight and

9

puffed. Then he took another pull of beer.

'Hey, barkeep! What you trying to do — poison me with this stuff?'

Ed Kirby paled. While some people reddened when their gorge rose, Ed Kirby went almost white and his eyes protruded slightly. He had gone behind the counter and was reaching for a cleaning rag. He flung the rag down and glanced at Johnny Carver.

'What do I do with that hobo?'

'It's your beer, Ed,' the deputy remarked philosophically.

'You figure it's bad?'

'Might be a mistake to ask me to judge, Ed. I've been drinking it for so long now I mightn't be able to tell the difference.'

Kirby's eyes narrowed. 'You're rattled,' he accused softly. 'He's got you rattled as well, by grab!'

'You're wrong, pard,' Johnny smiled. 'I'm not a bit rattled. Go see what he wants before he goes up in smoke.'

Kirby cleared the end of the bar and

reluctantly approached the stranger at the table. 'Mister, I've just got one thing to say to you: if you don't like the beer in here you'd better go someplace else.'

'Oh!' The lean, teak-dark face assumed an ugly cast. The deep-set eyes darted to the straight, square shoulders of Johnny Carver, fused with Johnny's eyes in the back-bar mirror. 'So you want me to go somewhere else, eh?'

'There's half a dozen other saloons in town,' Ed Kirby informed him. 'You might get what you want in one of them.'

'So you've got the gall to call this stuff beer.'

'It's what it is. And I don't want any trouble from you.'

'Is that a fact?' the other sneered. 'Come over here, buster.' And when Ed Kirby was close enough, a stream of beer was dashed into his face.

The bartender mouthed an oath and lunged at his tormentor, only to be brought up short by the dark muzzle of a Remington .44.

'No rough stuff, mister,' the stranger chided with a chuckle. 'Now, you go wipe your face and then fetch me a real beer.'

'The hell I will!' Ed Kirby panted. He swung to the deputy sheriff. 'Johnny, are you going to let him get away with this?'

Johnny shrugged and crossed the floor without haste. He noted the raw challenge in the stranger's flaring eyes. The muzzle of the Remington shifted fractionally so that it was pointing at the lawman's midriff. The lanky man eased in his chair, teeth bared in a grin of amusement.

'You're the local star-packer, I see. Well, friend, you ought to make a law against these fellas trying to poison their customers.'

The steady gun muzzle started an odd tingle along Johnny's nerves. It was the first time he had ever had a gun pointed at him in this fashion. The experience was frightening. He dipped his head slowly. 'I never thought of that,' he murmured. 'Might be a good idea, when you come to think of it, Ed. After all, the customer is usually right.'

'What's the matter with you?' Kirby almost screamed. 'Are you turning yellow, Johnny?'

'Now, that ain't fair, Ed,' the deputy admonished. 'No call to get yourself in a steam. Isn't that so, mister?'

The stranger flung his head back and laughed. 'Me? Why, I go plumb along with you, youngster.'

'Deputy, if you please, sir. Name of Johnny Carver.'

'Pleased to meet you, Carver. My name's Bannon, Lute Bannon.'

'Howdy, Lute . . . Ed, you bring the man another beer, like he said.'

'What!' Ed Kirby howled. 'Are you out of your mind? You mean you're going to lick his boots? Hell, Johnny, when folks hear about this, you'll be — '

'Close your yap and bring the gent another beer,' the deputy insisted. '*Go do it, you damn fool!*'

Kirby swallowed and backed off to the counter. He glanced at the batwing doors as though hoping someone might arrive and rescue him from this humiliation. He used his rag to wipe his face. His hands trembled as he drew another beer.

In the meantime, Johnny drew up a chair across the table from the stranger. Lute Bannon nodded approval and wiped his nose on his shirt-sleeve. He made himself more comfortable, then licked the index finger of his left hand and traced a line along the barrel of his .44. It was as though he had noticed a speck of dust that offended him.

'You'll have a drink with me, Deputy?' The tone implied that Johnny Carver would refuse at his peril.

'Why not, Lute?' Johnny said easily. 'Only, I get nervous drinking with a man holding a shooting iron on me. Say, what are you scared of, Lute?'

'Me scared! Blazes, I'm not scared, sonny. Ain't nothing in this burg to make a man scared. You ain't figuring

14

to run me in, I hope?'

'Nothing could be further from my mind, Lute.'

Bannon emitted a hee-haw of a laugh. He slapped the table forcefully. 'A drink for the lawjohn as well, barkeep. And hurry it up, will you, boy?'

He twirled the Remington so that the sunlight filtering through the window caught it and was reflected dully from the blued steel of the barrel. Then he made a final flourish that set the weapon firmly in its pouch.

'Well, I guess — ' Lute Bannon broke off and his lantern jaw went slack. A garbled oath spilled through the growth of whisker around his lips. 'I'll be damned! I've been stupid enough to ask a sidewinder to have a drink with me . . . '

What amazed him most was the way Johnny Carver's Colt had materialised in his hand, and the subtlety of the movement that trained the muzzle on a spot between the stranger's eyes. Ed

Kirby sucked a hard breath and let a schooner of beer spill from his fingers.

'Climb to your feet, Lute,' the deputy urged softly. 'Real gentle now.'

'Hey, you just wait a minute, you two-timing tin-packer!'

'Get up, Lute,' Johnny insisted. '*Pronto*, or I'll be obliged to give you a third peeper.'

Lute Bannon did as he was told. On his feet, he gave his chair a vicious backwards kick that sent it across the floor. He eyed the younger man balefully. 'I got something to say to you, mister,' he said in a vibrant croak. 'You're going to be very sorry.'

'Get moving, pard.'

When Bannon had taken a couple of steps, Johnny told him to halt and quickly relieved him of his weapon and pushed it under his waistband.

'Ed . . . ' Johnny said. 'Bring me a beer. Just one, Ed.'

'Sure, Johnny,' Kirby crowed hysterically. 'Anything you say, Johnny.'

'Now wait!' Lute Bannon snarled.

'I'm not taking any funny stuff from you, Deputy. You're barking up the wrong tree.'

'I'm not barking anywhere,' Johnny protested. 'All I aim to do is tie a can to a scraggy dog's tail.'

'The hell you are!'

'Freeze, or I'll drill you, boy.'

Johnny took the foaming schooner that Kirby handed him and flung the contents into Bannon's face. Then, before the stranger could collect himself, he pouched his gun and swung his balled right fist. It hit Lute Bannon with the force of a sledgehammer and lifted him high on his runover bootheels. Bannon appeared to poise in mid-air for the space of five seconds, then he buckled at the knees and tumbled into the sawdust.

Johnny Carver grabbed him by the scruff of the neck. 'Guess I'll shut you up in a cage until you cool off, Lute.' And to the open-mouthed bartender: 'Ed, I'd be pleased if you'd hold the door open for me.'

2

A search of the prisoner, conducted by Sheriff Hab Beely, disclosed nothing more than the average range rider might be expected to carry. Lute Bannon had twenty dollars on his person and there was no one around to deny his assertion that this represented the dog-end of two months' wages from the last ranch he had worked for. Still, Johnny Carver was of the opinion that it had been more than two months since Bannon had been involved in anything as mundane as cow-punching.

He and Hab left the obstreperous stranger in the care of Buck Arden, the jailer, and bent their steps towards Darton's saloon once more. The sheriff was in need of a drink and so was Johnny. A group of admiring townsfolk pressed into the bar room behind them, eager to hear from the lips of Ed Kirby

— or, better still, from Johnny himself — exactly how he had bluffed the fractious newcomer and turned the tables on him.

The bartender declared he had done all the talking he felt obliged to do, but he added for the benefit of those who had not already heard his eulogy: 'I ain't going to repeat it any more. Johnny Carver made one of the nerviest plays I ever saw in my life. Then he hit that bird so hard he didn't know if it was Christmas or Thanksgiving. The funny thing was,' Kirby added with an apologetic grin, 'I thought at first that Johnny was going to play chicken and let him wreck the place. But not Johnny Carver! Now if I was asked for my opinion about — '

'All right, Ed,' Johnny Carver interrupted with a grin. 'No call to give these folks the notion they're going to have to fork out money for a medal. What do you say we just let it pass?'

Johnny and the sheriff took their beers to the table by the wall where

Lute Bannon had sat. The sheriff found a button on a chair that must have broken loose from the stranger's shirt. It might come in handy, he thought, and put it away carefully in the pocket of his own shirt. He eyed the younger man with uneasy amusement.

'You're going to be a hero now, it looks like, mister. Come next election, they'll want to fit you up with my badge.'

'That's not a bit funny, Hab,' Johnny chided. 'I don't want your job. Fact is,' he added slowly, 'I've been getting the feeling lately to climb into the saddle of a cowpony and do some real work.'

'Oh!' Beely murmured in a tone that signified he had guessed the real reason for the statement.

'What do you mean, 'Oh', Hab?' Johnny's tanned cheeks took on a darker tinge. 'Sam Ford's got all the riders he needs at the minute, so you might as well forget it.'

'Forget what?' Beely needled with a fat chuckle. 'That Sam Ford's got all the punchers he needs? Maybe he has, youngster, but what Sam hasn't got is a husband for that pretty gal of his.'

'Come off it, Hab.' Johnny's eyes had a reflective glint. 'When Ginny Ford wants a husband she won't ask her dad to find her one. She's got a mind of her own.'

'Yeah, and a keen, purty eye in her head, boy. That same eye is on you, and you know it fine. If I was in your boots I'd feel the proudest gent ever to come west of the Missouri. But let me be serious for a minute. You're earning more with that badge on your shirt than Sam could pay you for eating dust. Oh, I know he won't live for ever, and the gent who puts a ring on Ginny's finger will likely rest his boots on Sam's office desk some day.'

'You're still joshing, Hab,' Johnny scowled. 'You've got a mean streak in you some place that'll have to be flushed out before you're fitten company.'

'You're wrong, boy,' the sheriff

objected with relish. 'But I guess I am guilty of meddling in your affairs. But you know damn well I wish you luck, whatever you do.'

'Sure. And thanks, Hab.'

'Right.' Beely became brisk. 'Go fetch me another beer. And tell Ed to give you a couple of prime cigars.'

Beely smoked a pipe and rarely used cigars or cigarettes, but he lit up a fine Cuban perfecto with relish when his deputy rejoined him. Johnny brought only one beer, for Hab, saying he had drunk enough. He advised the sheriff to consider what had happened to Burt Mageby, who used to own the Rafter M, out on the north fork of the Antelope. Mageby had drunk himself into ruination and finished up in 'an early grave'.

Hab Beely chuckled as he took a swallow of beer and wiped the froth on the cuff of his shirt. He went on puffing at the cigar, but Johnny could see the soberness that presently edged into the sheriff's good humour. Yes, there was something on Hab's mind, he realised. But it was easy to guess what: it had to do with Lute Bannon, whose bony claybank was at the livery stable, feeding on oats, and whose gun was lodged in a drawer at the law office.

Johnny splayed a hand on the table top and considered the long, capable fingers. 'You don't like that fella turning up the way he did?'

'You're right,' the sheriff admitted after a short pause. 'I've got this feeling again that I've had for quite a while now.'

Johnny struck a match for his cigar. 'Bannon's just a drifter, likely. He's playing a solo game, and we can handle him. Maybe he can handle that .44 he likes playing with, but a day or two in a cage will bring him to his senses. He figured he could drop in on a quiet little burg and throw his weight round. He got a lesson, and there's no more to it.'

'I hope you're right,' Sheriff Beely said with a sigh. He finished his beer. 'But why did he pick on Ed after you went into the saloon?'

'Coincidence, maybe. Nothing else, surely? You suggesting he wanted to get my size?'

'*Our* size, maybe. I saw the way he looked at me when he drifted into town. I might have been a pile of hay for the way he sniggered. You found nothing much in his saddlebags, and that crowbait isn't branded. Even so — '

'It mightn't add up to anything much.'

'I think it adds up to something.' Beely re-lit his cigar. 'Consider: a hardcase on a run-down nag. But it was a good nag when he set out from his starting point. All it needs is a day or so at the livery, stoking up on hay and grain. Now, you know what they say about a gent who neglects his horse?'

'Sure. I'd like to kick him for that. All right, I'll go back to the jailhouse and have a talk with Bannon. Maybe I can make a deal with him. I could promise him early release if he gives us a bit of his past history and a hint of his plans for the future.'

Hab Beely lifted his shoulders in a dubious shrug. 'You're more optimistic than I am, son. But go right ahead if you want to.'

Johnny left the sheriff, chewing over what he had said. When he reached the law office he was greeted with a burst of discordant song.

'I've travelled long and I've
travelled far,
And I've never met a gal who
looked like Lil . . .
Says I to her, 'My fair young
maid,
We're going to travel right over
that hill,
We're going to travel right over
that hill!' . . . '

He found Buck Arden holding his hands over his ears.

'Tell that hyena to sing under his breath, Johnny. If he gives with one more verse I'll go plumb crazy.'

Johnny stifled a tight grin and went through to the cell block. Lute Bannon had been stretched out on his cot, but at sight of the deputy he crossed to the bars. His smile had the intent of a naked dagger.

'I want to talk to you, buster,' he announced gravely. His right eye had a curious habit of shuttling across to the left one, but Johnny saw it as an attempt to shield his virulent hatred. This would be a bad one to turn your back on, he decided.

'That's good,' Johnny commended. 'The sooner you talk, the sooner we'll get to the bottom of this.'

'The bottom of what, lawman?'

'The way you hit town. The way you set about treeing Ed Kirby. Kirby doesn't take kindly to being treed by strangers. What's the jig, Lute?'

Bannon indicated the tip of his chin. 'You pack a mean wallop, sonny. I never forget a gent who slugs me like that.'

'You asked for it, Lute.'

'Did I now?' Bannon coughed and spat through the bars so that Johnny had to shift his boot quickly. A slow anger began to simmer. There was no point in using soft-glove tactics here; Luke Bannon was snake-mean and as treacherous as any sidewinder.

'You'd better brush up on your manners, friend. I can keep you locked up without chuck or water for a month. Nobody would even know you're here.'

'Trying to scare me, huh?' the lean man sneered. 'Now, you hear this good, Mr Deputy: Stockwell is just a hick town with a lot of old ladies running things. You'd rather I was fifty miles away than right here, gracing your flea-trap jail. You admit that, don't you?'

'Sure, I do,' Johnny told him. 'But let's get started on the right foot. Who are you?'

'I done told you. Name of Lute Bannon. Say, fella, what did you do with my shooting iron?'

'It's safe enough.'

27

'What about my nag?'

'Getting some flesh on its bones,' Johnny rejoined coldly. The neglected horse was a touchy subject with him. 'You rode it plumb into the ground. Never stopped much to feed or water it. You certainly hit these parts in a hurry, Lute. Where from, is what I'd like to know?'

'You know what happened to the curious cat?' Bannon reminded him, making his eyes squint in that odd fashion. 'How long are you going to keep me locked up?'

'That's for the sheriff to decide.'

'Ahuh! But a gent can get out if he pays a fine, can't he? How much will it cost to get me out of here?'

Johnny pretended to consider. 'Let's see . . . For what you got up to, I guess maybe fifty dollars. But we might make it easier if you tell me where you hailed from and why you landed in this burg.'

'Fifty dollars you say? No haggling?'

'Wouldn't matter. You've only got twenty dollars. Not a gent in town

28

would go bail for you. So you'd better answer my questions.'

'You do something for me, Tin Star,' Bannon said in a confidential whisper. 'You go clear to hell and then tell me what it's like there.'

He turned his back and lay down on the cot. He cradled his head and crossed his legs. His voice lifted defiantly.

'So there we was, just Lil and me,
Over that hill and riding free.
Says I to her, 'My fair young maid,
You and me is gonna get wed . . .''

Buck Arden swore. 'He's going to drive me *loco*, Johnny. I'm liable to shoot him if he don't shut up.'

'Just pretend he isn't there,' Johnny advised absently. He was heading for the street when he heard a buckboard rattle up to the front of the law office and stop.

A minute later a golden-skinned, dark-haired girl of nineteen or twenty came into the hallway. She was dressed in levis and checkered shirt, the one obvious concession to her femininity the white silk scarf she wore loosely around her throat. Yet the girl was entirely feminine — full-bosomed and soft-lipped. Her blue eyes flashed in a manner that caused Johnny's heart to skip a beat.

Lute Bannon had stopped singing. The lanky man was back at the cell bars and, like Buck Arden, appeared totally fascinated by this vision of beauty and breath of prairie freshness. A low, appreciative whistle escaped Bannon.

The visitor gave the prisoner back in the cell block a single glance before concentrating on the deputy. 'I came to town to do an errand for Dad, Johnny,' she began. 'So I thought I'd look you up. I saw Hab along the street, and he said you might be busy . . . '

'He is busy, ma'am,' Lute Bannon informed her dolefully. 'He's treating me something awful in here. Say, Miss,

30

I — uh — didn't catch your name, ma'am.'

'My name is Ginny Ford,' the girl supplied with a slight nod in Bannon's direction.

'Well, is that so! A right pretty name it is, too, ma'am, if I may say so. Like I was going to tell you, this here *hombre* with the tin badge . . . '

Johnny's mouth firmed in grim lines and he took the girl's arm and led her out to the street. Behind them, Bannon launched into his song with a powerful delivery. Ginny Ford laughed, but she soon noticed the tight lines around the deputy's mouth.

'Who is he, Johnny?' she asked with a suppressed chuckle.

'A troublemaker, for sure,' Johnny gritted. 'Some stranger. Rode into town and made trouble in Darton's saloon.'

The girl sobered. She placed her hand on Johnny's arm, oblivious of the passers-by who stared at them. 'He looked mischievous to me, Johnny. He sounds mischievous as well. Did he come into town alone?'

'Thank heaven, he did,' Johnny said fervently. 'Three or four of his stripe and Hab and me would have a job on our hands. We'll give him a night in the cells to cool off, and I guess we'll send him out of town in the morning before the saloons open. But let's forget that jasper for a minute, Ginny. It's great to see you. Everything's all right at the ranch, I hope? Your dad's in good health?'

Ginny tossed her dark head and laughed. 'Dad never felt better. That's what he says. The spring round-up was a huge success, in his estimation. There never was such a crop of calves. The summer's hot enough, but there's plenty of water in the creeks, and — Oh, goodness, Johnny, there I go talking like a rancher's daughter! But you've been a cowhand yourself and you know how it is. You've never considered giving up that badge and becoming a rider again?'

It was his turn to laugh. 'Funny you

should say that. Yes, I play with the notion every so often. You get tired of living in a small hotel room, seeing the same dusty street in the mornings, the same faces you saw yesterday. I do get a yearning to sniff grass and sage and have a nimble cowpony under me. But where is this leading?' he asked with affected concern. 'Your dad isn't short of hands?'

'Short or not, you can get a job with Bar F any time you feel like it. Dad has said so often enough.'

Thus they chatted for five minutes or so. The initial interest shown by the gossips had waned. Ginny had to make a few purchases at Joe Dell's hardware store, and Johnny said he would collect them and load them in the rig. This done, he persuaded the girl to have a cup of coffee with him in Ma Pearson's cafe. In all, he was in the girl's company for the better part of an hour before she resumed the seat of the buckboard, gave him a cheerful goodbye, and tooled the vehicle out of town.

Hab Beely was back on his bench in the shade of the law office awning when Johnny retraced his steps to the building. Lute Bannon had quietened and Beely declared he had threatened him with starvation if he didn't stop 'that awful caterwauling'.

Johnny had expected something more rewarding in his absence. 'You got nothing out of him besides his name and the song about Lil?'

'What did you expect?' the fat man grunted. 'I figured I might find his name or his dial in that bunch of old dodgers we have. But if he's wanted anywhere I've no information on it.'

Johnny scratched the nape of his neck. He thought Hab should have tried a little harder. 'So what do we do with him?' he asked.

'Let him spend a night behind bars and see if it cools his courage.' The sheriff added sententiously: 'I've seen a lot of tough *hombres* end up begging to get out from behind bars. Anyhow, in the morning we'll mount him up and send him on his way.'

And that would settle it, Johnny thought sourly. He mentioned how Bannon had spoken of a fine, and the sum he had stated. At which Hab Beely resumed his earlier worried look.

'He's a queer bird and no mistake, Johnny. But why did he pick our town to find a perch?'

'Why?' Johnny echoed. Perhaps they were investing Lute Bannon with more importance than he warranted. Then he recalled that well-cared for gun in the desk drawer and fingered his jawline. He doubted that Lute Bannon's visit to Stockwell could be written off as pure chance. There was something else behind it that would be revealed in due course. Next, Johnny recalled the lanky man's remark concerning Ginny Ford and repressed a shudder.

Watching him, Hab Beely reached for his pipe and tobacco pouch. Hab was glad he had taken on a man of the calibre of Johnny Carver. Hab shared the apprehension he knew his deputy

was pretending to conceal. But was there really anything to be afraid of, he wondered. Had he and Johnny been insulated from trouble for so long that the arrival of a wild-looking drifter was enough to bring them out in a sweat?

'Look yonder,' Johnny said suddenly, pointing to the west end of the street. 'See what I see?'

'What is it?' Beely demanded. 'A gent riding into town? You *are* getting jittery, boy.' His voice rose to an unusually high pitch. 'We're behaving like a couple of ladies from the sewing circle, do you know that?'

'Another stranger, Hab,' Johnny droned. 'Would you like to make a small bet, old-timer?'

'Bet?' Beely snorted. 'Are you going out of your mind, boy! What sort of bet?'

'I'm ready to lay odds that this bird coming along the street is a pard of the specimen we've got locked up in jail.'

3

The second stranger to ride into town that day was a short, thickset man who rode a grey horse that looked as tired and neglected as the beast Lute Bannon had been riding. He moved down the road at an unhurried pace, glancing from side to side as though searching for something or somebody. Johnny Carver knew well enough what he was searching for. The squat man and Lute Bannon had planned to rendezvous in Stockwell. Bannon had ventured in first to test the water, having made arrangements to meet this second scarecrow. But what did they have in mind on the resumption of their relationship?

While Johnny was asking himself this question the stranger was gradually drawing level with him and Hab Beely. Johnny was surprised when the sheriff stepped into the roadway, directly into the path of the weary grey horse.

The rider failed to notice him until the last second, then he hauled down hard to keep the horse from blundering into Hab. Even so, the stout sheriff was taken off balance a trifle and grabbed the grey's reins close to the bit to steady himself.

'What's going on?' the newcomer demanded. 'It's the law, by grab!' he answered himself. 'What's the big idea, Sheriff?'

'I'd like a word with you, friend,' Hab said on a reedy note.

Johnny was convinced that the sheriff was using the wrong tack. But he had made his play and he might need some backing, so Johnny rose from the bench and stood on the edge of the plank sidewalk so that he could study the newcomer more closely. He saw a round, blunt-nosed face that was half-hidden by the downturned brim of his hat. The heavy jowls were darkened with a week's growth of stubble. The checkered shirt the man wore was far too tight for his stomach girth. The buckskin vest had trouble accommodating the breadth of the chest and shoulders. A Winchester rifle was snugged slantwise into the saddle boot and a .45 Colt hung at his right side. Still, there was nothing about him to suggest he was anything but a drifting cowhand on his way through. Beely should have waited for any possible developments before acting.

'You want to gab with me?' the squat man said with a trace of wry amusement in his voice. 'Somebody told me this was a quiet burg, with a reasonable man rodding the law. What would you like to talk about, though?'

His blunt approach served to take some of the steam out of the sheriff and he seemed nonplussed for a moment. Then he cleared his throat in an authoritative growl. 'What handle do you go by, friend?'

'Me? Well, if you really must know, Sheriff, my name's Post. Fred Post. Happens to be my real name,' he added laconically while weighing up the deputy standing behind the badge-packer. 'Say, did somebody steal something around here?' he added with a chuckle.

'Not so far.' Hab Beely refused to acknowledge any opening for levity. 'Where do you hail from, Post?'

'Well, I'll be dogged!' the other commented, continuing to stare at Johnny Carver. 'Here I am, hungry and tired as a wore-out coyote, and you want to know where I hail from! Say, what about that, youngster?'

Johnny said nothing and Hab Beely insisted: 'Where from, mister?'

'Why, from just about any place you mention, that's where.' He pushed his hat away from his brow and cuffed his forehead. The eyes were as alert as a hawk's. 'It's the best I can tell you, Sheriff, take it or leave it. Anything else you hanker to know?'

Beely reached the conclusion belatedly that he had, indeed, acted impulsively. But the damage was done

40

and he ploughed on in his characteristically straightforward fashion. 'We've an ordinance about vagrants,' he reminded Fred Post. 'A day and a night is the limit. After that you'd better — '

'Vagrant!' the squat man echoed with a hard laugh. He fumbled in a pocket and produced a worn wallet. He leaned towards the sheriff to let him see a wad of bills tucked away in there. 'Does that let me pass, Sheriff? You'd like me to strip to see which brand I'm wearing?'

Johnny thought of checking for a neck brand on the grey, but something made him hold his hand. Let Hab finish what he had started.

Beely released his grip on the reins and stepped back. 'Go ahead then,' he said curtly.

'Well, I'll be!' Post put an agonised grin on Johnny. 'Know something, youngster? Strikes me this burg ain't what it's drummed up to be. Has a bunch of robbers been here lately?'

Still Johnny remained on the sidelines and left it to Hab to retort: 'You

41

go ahead, mister, like I said.'

When the thickset stranger called Fred Post had gigged his horse on down the street, Hab Beely shrugged and muttered a curse. 'Don't remind me that I might have blundered,' he warned. 'Made a damn fool of myself, didn't I?'

Johnny continued to watch Fred Post's progress along the dusty road. 'It was your play, I guess. But I'd have given him time to light and look around. He'll be on his guard now.'

The sheriff frowned at that. 'Then you really do think there's something queer about these two birds coming here?'

Johnny didn't answer immediately. He watched Fred Post draw up at the rail fronting Saul Darton's saloon. Hab Beely shared his interest. Just as Lute Bannon had done, Post mounted the plankwalk and peered all around him. His gaze touched the two lawmen, and Johnny growled when he spat deliberately. Then Post hitched his gunbelt up

42

on his girth and breasted the batwing doors.

Johnny released a soft whistle. 'Sure has a familiar look to it, Hab. Bannon went in there and picked a row with the barkeep. But I figure that was because he spotted my badge and wanted to size me up.'

'Did you see the roll of money?' Beely marvelled. 'Enough to choke a mule. Where did he get it?'

'We'll keep an eye on the bozo,' Johnny said with a firm nod. He was really worried at this juncture, sensing that a heavy shadow was forming which might threaten the whole town. He tried to shrug the feeling off. 'Look, I'll ease along to Darton's and see what's what.'

'Go easy,' the sheriff advised. 'I'll hold back till I get a shout.'

'Won't be no call to shout,' Johnny returned with a tight grin.

There were a dozen or so customers in the saloon when Johnny eased through the batwings and halted to peer around him. The man called Fred Post was at the far end of the counter, a bottle and a glass in front of him, in the act of tipping a splash of whisky into the glass. He had noticed the deputy's arrival but appeared carelessly indifferent. Johnny moved to the counter and caught Ed Kirby's eye.

'Beer, Ed.'

'You're sure making up for lost time,' Kirby commented. 'Glad you're here. You've seen the fat party who just came in?'

'I see him.'

His beer drawn, Johnny brought the schooner to the table where Lute Bannon had sat earlier. He took a swallow and fished for his tobacco sack and papers. He was putting a cigarette together when boots scraped over the floor and he lifted his head to see Fred Post.

Post had the bottle and glass with him and placed them on the table. 'Mind if I join you, Deputy?'

'No law says you can't.'

'Beer your poison? Go ahead and take a swig of this stuff. It ain't all that bad.'

'No, thanks,' Johnny declined as the squat man sat down heavily, making the chair creak. Johnny ran his tongue along the edge of the wheatstraw paper, rolled it and placed the cylinder between his lips. The tolerant smile that usually played around his mouth was absent. 'What can I do for you?' he queried.

'Depends on what you might be able to do for me, I guess,' the other answered slowly. His eyes were like large black beads that rolled around lazily. He grinned, turning the palms of his hands upwards. They were wide hands, with spatulate fingers. If he had ever used them for roping cattle out of brush, it had been a long time ago. 'Your sheriff don't cotton to me, I reckon. What did he think I was, anyhow?'

'Hab?' Johnny's mouth relented fractionally. He let a wisp of smoke trickle

45

out. 'He's just careful, I suppose. Stockwell's been a quiet town for years. It's the way Hab likes it. It's the way I like it.'

'Ahuh! A quiet town. Well, I'm glad to hear it, Deputy. What did you say your handle was?'

'I didn't say. But it's Carver. Johnny Carver. My friends call me Johnny.'

'I see.' A suggestion of mild contempt edged into Post's voice. 'Then I'll call you Johnny as well, I guess. But you strike me as a more reasonable critter than the sheriff. Maybe I'll get more out of you than I'll get out of him.'

He left his meaning hanging in the air and Johnny refrained from pressing for an explanation. 'What about your nag outside?' he asked instead.

'Hell yes! Plumb forgot my horse. A man who forgets his horse is a fool, huh?'

'It's easy forgetting things.'

The thickset man had another drink and smacked his lips. 'Say, that ain't bad at all.'

'Your partner figured the beer wasn't so good.'

Fred Post betrayed a start; a frown puckered his brow. 'My partner, you say? I'm not following you too well.'

It had been a shot in the dark but it had gone home well enough. Johnny knew by the way the beady eyes rolled briefly. He took a drag on his cigarette, dropped it to the floor, and planted his bootheel on it. He met Post's puzzled stare blandly.

'Maybe I'm mistaken. Maybe you haven't got a partner?'

'Happens I have. But — '

'You lost him somewhere along the trail? Got separated, maybe?'

'How did you know? Are we talking about different people?'

'I don't think so,' Johnny replied coolly. 'This party is pretty thin, with a queer eye and a bit of a bend in the shoulders. Rides a claybank.'

'Yeah! That sounds like him. Did you hear a name?'

'Calls himself Lute Bannon.'

'Old Lute! Good gravy . . . What about that now! Yeah, Lute and me split up a while back. I wondered where he'd gotten to. You say he's in town? But no, you didn't. Did he drift on through?'

'He's in the hoosegow,' Johnny informed him gently. 'Behind bars. He happened along here and fussed something awful over the beer.'

'Lute in jail?' Fred Post echoed in wonder. 'But the Lute I'm speaking of wouldn't hurt a fly. He must have been under the weather. What's the charge anyway?'

'You might call it breaking the peace,' Johnny suggested. 'You see, this is a real quiet town, and we like it that way. But to get back to what you were saying a minute ago. You thought I might be able to do something for you?'

'Yes, I did. You see, Lute and me and a couple other fellas spent a while over in Nevada. We made it pretty good, hunting wild horses. Then we decided we'd get ourselves a nice little cattle spread and settle down. Any place like that in your territory?'

It happened that Johnny did know of such a place. The old Benson ranch in Mulehead Valley had lain idle for three years — ever since Tad Benson died, without kith or kin. Tad had been paying off the mortgage on the ranch, and when he died the stock had been sold to help meet the note. The ranch could be bought cheaply enough, but Johnny did not feel disposed to tell Post about Mulehead Valley. If the squat man turned out to be anything like Lute Bannon, the country would be better off without them.

'You might see Ray Glover,' he told Post, knowing he would be able to unearth this knowledge easily enough. 'He's the land agent. But you'd have to fork out ready money.'

'How much do you figure? And for what sort of place?'

'That's not my line,' Johnny said with a niggling of worry. 'You'd have to see Glover himself.' He straightened his hat and rose. Fred Post asked him to wait.

'What about my pard, Deputy? He could get on the right side of the jail bars if a fine was paid?'

'Maybe so,' Johnny agreed. 'You'd better take that up with Sheriff Beely.'

'I'll do that, mister,' Post said warmly. 'You've been a big help.'

The note of condescension in his voice annoyed the deputy, but he swallowed a sour taste and left the saloon.

A little later he was sitting out front of the law office, telling Hab Beely what had transpired in Darton's. The sheriff looked stricken when he learned that Bannon and Post might be going into ranching together.

'I sure as hell don't like the sound of it, boy. I can see that you don't neither. I don't believe they ever hunted or broke a horse in their lives. They're up to something that's got nothing to do with raising cattle.'

'But why did Bannon put on that act to get himself locked up?' Johnny pondered. 'All the signs say he wanted it to happen.'

'Why?' Hab Beely murmured. 'He wanted to try us out, see how we'd handle a roughneck? Well, if that was his game he knows the answer. We're not a couple of easy marks for the first hardcase that happens along.'

'But we can't hold Bannon for long,' Johnny reminded him. 'Bannon asked about a fine, and if he can't make it, his friend can.'

'I know,' Beely nodded. 'I'd better see Judge Maxwell. In the meantime, keep an eye on Post, Johnny.'

'I'll watch him,' Johnny Carver promised.

Around the middle of the day, he and Hab were eating lunch in Ma Pearson's cafe when the screen door was thrust open and the squat man called Fred Post came through. Post just nodded to the lawmen and took a table close to the door. He was half-way through his meal by the time Johnny and the sheriff rose to leave. Post spoke to Hab Beely as he passed his table.

'Oh, Sheriff, I'd like to see you about getting my pard out of the lock-up. You set a fine yet?'

'You can see me in my office in an hour,' Beely informed him curtly. 'I'll have a word with the judge.' And on the street he erupted with uncharacteristic vehemence: 'They're sure as Hades planning something, boy. I can smell it in the air. I can feel it in my bones. Only thing we can do with these gents is tell them to leave town *pronto* and not come back.'

'Sure,' Johnny said drily. 'But will they do that? They might leave right enough, but what's to hinder them coming back later and raising hell?'

'You got a better idea?' Hab asked with desperation in his voice.

'Maybe. I'd say we should go along with them till we see what game they're playing.'

'You might be right,' Beely conceded. 'No call to borrow trouble until it comes. But supposing they have more pards hanging around? What happens if they all come visiting?'

It was a possibility that had already occurred to Johnny Carver, and there was no point in saying the prospect didn't worry him. He had heard of an Arizona town that had been taken over by outlaws. There had been a hectic reign of terror before outside help was recruited, but by then a lot of blood had been spilled and a lot of damage done.

'We'll take one fence at a time,' he suggested with more confidence than he felt. 'Else we'll end up afraid to sleep in bed nights.'

Hab left him, saying something about seeing the judge, and urging him to keep his 'eyes peeled better than ever'. Johnny began what appeared a leisurely patrol of the streets and returned to Main as Fred Post came oozing out of Pearson's cafe, smoking a cigar. If the stranger noticed the deputy he gave no indication. He swung off to the nearest saloon and passed inside. Johnny was tempted to follow him, but it might be the very reaction the squat man expected.

He made his way to the livery stable instead, to check on the stranger's grey horse. It had been lodged in a stall alongside Lute Bannon's claybank and the hostler told him he had been ordered to get both animals back into shape.

'That fat bird didn't say when he'd want the nags, Ben?'

The elderly hostler shook his grizzled head. 'Town's sure getting popular with strangers of a sudden,' he opined. 'But you know something, Johnny?'

'What?' Johnny queried and waited. Ben Shaw had a sharp eye in his head and might have something important to say.

'Well, take a look at the grey's shoes.' Shaw raised the hind hooves and gestured. 'Worn thin as blazes. The claybank's are in the same state. These nags have been ridden a long ways, Johnny. Fellas that own them could be on the run, don't you figure?'

'Maybe,' was Johnny's taut response. 'Funny, too, that they're not branded. But don't say anything to anybody else.'

He was more thoughtful than ever as he retraced his steps to the main street. He saw Hab Beely on his accustomed bench at the front of the law office, hat tilted forward and pipe in mouth. He was about to ask the sheriff if he wanted a cushion when the fat man jerked his head.

'That jasper Post's at the land office, boy. So he wasn't bluffing about looking for a ranch. His horse tell you anything?'

'No brand. Ben Shaw noticed how both horses are practically walking on their bare feet. Post wasn't on again about paying Bannon's fine?'

'Not yet. Judge thinks we've both got the jitters and there's no real grounds for holding Bannon after he fines him.'

Johnny's jaw hardened. 'Then we'll just have to play our own game, Hab. And that means playing it cool, like these two *hombres* are doing.'

4

Johnny was on the side of the street opposite the land office when the heavy-set man called Fred Post reappeared. Johnny had positioned himself in a doorway where he could watch Ray Glover's quarters without being seen by anyone leaving the office. He saw Post rock to a halt on the edge of the sidewalk, cheroot drooping from his lips while he took in the busy scene around him. Then he stepped into the roadway, ducked past a flat-bottomed wagon with a rawboned farmer on the driving seat, and set a course for the law office.

Johnny considered tracking Post, just in case he made things too hot for Hab to handle on his own, but he decided to wait until he heard what the land agent had to say about his caller.

★ ★ ★

Ray Glover was a thin, balding, shifty-eyed man who was reputed to have made more money out of real estate than any cattleman on the range could hope to make out of a lifetime in the ranching business. But Glover's appearance belied any desire for the good things that money could buy. He had been wearing the same old clawhammer coat for years; the collar and cuffs of his shirt were always in need of darning. His one visible concession to luxury related to the thick, fragrant cigars he smoked. He was a man in his late fifties, greying, but with steely blue eyes that were bright and alert.

A clerk showed the deputy through to the land agent's office, and when Johnny was announced Ray Glover smiled and rose to extend a lean right hand that was surprisingly cold to the touch. He invited Johnny to be seated and offered him a cigar from the engraved box that was always conveniently available. The deputy seated,

Glover sank down on his own swivel chair at the back of the huge polished desk that was the room's dominant feature.

'Isn't often I have the pleasure of your company, Johnny,' was his somewhat whimsical greeting. His voice was soft and had an odd musical quality that easily won him friends. 'Don't tell me you're thinking of chucking in your badge and taking up the cow business?'

Johnny chuckled obligingly, then sobered. 'Not yet, Mr Glover. You had a visitor a short while ago that I'm interested in.'

'Oh? Well, I might have known! That bird calls himself Fred Post. He's a rank stranger to these parts, isn't he?'

Johnny agreed that he was. He struck a match for the thick cigar and came to the point. 'I don't like prying into your business, sir, but this is an unusual situation . . .'

'I see.' Glover's blue eyes glinted with curiosity. 'You'd like to know what he wanted with me? You're keeping an eye on him?'

'You could put it that way. I've talked with Post, and he indicated he might be interested in buying a ranch. Did he ask you about a ranch?'

'Yes, he did, as a matter of fact. I've got nothing on my books at the moment but the old Benson place in Mulehead Valley. I told Post so. He was anxious to know how far it is from town. I explained that it was about six miles or so. He appeared to like the idea.'

'You mean he bought it?' Johnny asked hoarsely.

'Not right off. But he is plenty interested, and I admit I'd be glad to get that place off my hands. If somebody doesn't move in there mighty soon there won't be a wall standing or a yard of ground not covered in weeds. I bought the mortgage from the bank, you know, with an eye to making a modest profit.'

Johnny knew all that. 'So Post is

coming back again?' he asked.

'He said he'll look at the place and get in touch in a day or so.'

'I see.' Johnny told himself he ought to be relieved to hear this news, indicating as it did that Fred Post and his partner Bannon must really intend going into ranching. All the same, a doubt persisted. He prided himself on being a pretty sound judge of human nature and, no matter how he viewed it, he was unable to see Post and Bannon spending the rest of their days raising cattle.

Raising hell would be more like it.

'Is anything wrong, Johnny?' Ray Glover sounded concerned. 'If you've got something against this man I ought to be told about it.'

'What's the going price for the Benson place, Mr Glover?'

'Two thousand dollars. Yes, it's cheap, I know. But it'll take a lot of money to turn Mulehead Valley into a paying proposition.'

'I understand,' Johnny muttered. He

rose to go, the dead cigar between his fingers forgotten. 'Thanks for your help, sir.'

'A pleasure, Johnny. Say,' he added as the deputy reached the door, 'you're not planning on settling down yourself? I hear talk that — '

'Gossip,' Johnny interrupted with a grin. He opened the door, paused, and glanced back at the land agent. 'Supposing I did rustle up enough money to buy the Benson spread before Fred Post clinches the deal?'

'Bring me a healthy deposit and we'll talk turkey, Johnny. But you'll have to be mighty quick to beat Mr Post to it.' He laughed at his joke and Johnny nodded and closed the door behind him.

On the street he paused to run an elbow around the sweatband of his hat. His pulse was beating inordinately fast and he stood for a few minutes, mulling things over. He was convinced by now that Fred Post and his lanky pard wanted Mulehead Valley for a reason

61

that had little or nothing to do with ranching. But what other reason could there be?

'To serve as headquarters for some scheme they're hatching,' he mused excitedly. 'Why else?' The pair wanted a base convenient to town to lie low for a while. At two thousand dollars they would be getting the Benson place for a song. Also, they would have a ready-made cover for their real game, whatever that was . . .

* * *

Judge Aaron Maxwell had chosen to handle the matter of Lute Bannon differently from what the sheriff expected. The judge, a stickler for performing his duties according to the letter of the law, would settle for nothing less than a special court hearing to decide the case. He directed the sheriff to bring Lute Bannon to his chambers at the rear of the courthouse block. Fred Post tried to gain admittance to the hearing, but the judge decreed that the public would be excluded unless Bannon asked for a public hearing.

'What in hell is that?' the lanky man queried suspiciously. 'Now, lookit here, Judge, I ain't no greenhorn and don't you take me for one. You figuring on sending me to the pen? Because if you are — '

'Be quiet,' the portly judge admonished coldly. 'You can let me deal with your case here and now and get it over with, or you can apply for bail and wait a week or so until counsel can be hired to defend you.'

'This is the easiest way,' Hab Beely impressed on Bannon. 'Judge knows what he's doing, mister, and you'll be lucky to get off with a fine.'

'Well, that's different,' Bannon declared with a sardonic grin. 'Only, it had better not be too high, Sheriff. That deputy said — '

'Judge'll decide,' Beely inserted with finality.

Ed Kirby was brought from Saul Darton's saloon and the special court got under way. The hearing was brief and Judge Maxwell gave his ruling as soon as everyone concerned had given evidence.

'Thirty dollars, payable now, or stay in jail for seven days, sir.'

'Say, that's handsome of you, Judge,' Lute Bannon applauded. 'But I don't reckon I have thirty dollars on me at the minute. If you can wait — '

'Won't Fred Post pay your fine, Lute?' Johnny Carver broke in before Judge Maxwell could respond. 'Seeing as how he's your partner . . . '

'Oh, Fred'll pay, sure. But you wouldn't let him in, Deputy.'

The judge instructed Hab Beely to find Post at once and inform him of the condition set for Bannon's freedom. The sheriff, in turn, requested Johnny to fetch Fred Post. Johnny found the squat man in the street, leaning against a doorway, a matchstick between his teeth.

'Thirty dollars?' he echoed. 'Sure, I'll pay the bill for Lute. It means he'll get turned free right now?'

So saying he produced his wallet and peeled off the amount. Johnny's features were deadpan as he accepted the money and returned to the courthouse. The judge gave Bannon a receipt, and a short time later Johnny and the sheriff watched the two strangers head off along the road. Bannon had an arm resting on Fred Post's heavy shoulder, and his recital of his jail experience was punctuated with bursts of laughter. News of what was going on had leaked to the public at large and small groups of townspeople stared at the ill-assorted pair. When they turned in at the Stirrup saloon Hab Beely spat an oath.

'I've a hunch we let him off too easy. We should have got the judge to add a rider that those *hombres* leave town immediately.'

The sheriff's mood was soured even more when he learned that Fred Post had been to see Ray Glover about buying a cattle outfit. 'Only place for sale at the minute is the old Benson place in Mulehead Valley,' Johnny enlarged. 'Glover reckons Post will buy it before he's much older.'

Hab Beely ran his fingers through his hair. He viewed this development in much the same way as Johnny did.

'There's gents who work for a living and gents who don't,' he said musingly. 'Bannon and Post will do precious little work, I'll wager. What do you really figure, boy?'

Johnny shook his head and struck a match for the cigar he had taken from Ray Glover's place and which the sheriff eyed with some surprise. 'I don't rightly know, Hab,' he confessed, puffing the cigar alight. 'But I had a good look at Fred Post's hands. A man uses a rope for hunting wild horses, doesn't he?'

'What the devil else would he use?' the sheriff snorted peevishly. 'You're saying he's got soft hands?'

'Not exactly soft, but no rope burns.

66

No, sir, I can picture that gent with a six-shooter in his fist, but not a rope.'

'It's what I figure, too,' Beely sighed. 'But where are they going to get the *dinero* to buy the Benson spread?'

Johnny told him what the asking price was and what Glover had said about the old ranch needing a lot of money spent on it before it made a profit.

'Then, by gravy, there's got to be a catch to it.'

'It's what I figure, Hab. Glover said Post was pleased to hear the valley was pretty close to town. Maybe they are going into the cattle business, but I doubt it. First, Lute Bannon drifts into town, throws his weight around, and gets himself locked in jail. Then Fred Post turns up and goes looking for Bannon. Post admits that Bannon is his pard. More than that, he hints they might have other pards here and there — '

'Why did they separate before hitting town?' Beely queried worriedly.

'There could be a few reasons. Maybe they grew tired of each other's company and split up for a while. And they raised cain some place and hit out in different directions to make it difficult to track them. Or maybe their original idea was to pretend they were strangers — until they got the measure of the law here in Stockwell.'

'Why?' the sheriff insisted. 'I'm trying to figure what they're aiming to do when they stop their play-acting.'

Johnny shrugged. 'Your guess is as good as mine, Hab. But here's the point I want to make: they could be searching for a place to lie low for a spell. By and by their other pards might show up. The old Benson ranch would fill the bill for a gathering of the clans. They would be well away from town, but not all that far. I got to thinking before I left Glover's office. Two thousand is the going price for Benson's place. Well, I'm a thrifty gent and I've saved a bit, and as Mr Glover said he'd take a deposit — '

'You'd buy the Benson place to keep them from getting it?' Beely exclaimed. 'But that's a plumb crazy idea.'

'Not so crazy. I reckon it's a right good idea. I could get around to fixing up the house and barn in my spare time. Maybe, in a year or so, I could sell at a handsome profit. In the meantime, Post and his sidekick might go sour on the territory and decide to pull their stakes. You'd like that to happen?'

'By heck, I would, boy,' Beely said fervently. 'Look . . . they're leaving the Stirrup. They're heading this way. Let's duck in before they notice we're watching them. Damned if I want them to think I'm scared.'

It developed that Fred Post and Lute Bannon veered towards the alley leading to the livery stable. Then, a short time later, they emerged, Post on his grey and Bannon on his claybank. They went down the road at a walk and soon vanished beyond the town's western outskirts.

The sheriff said reedily: 'You reckon

they're really pulling out?'

'Wouldn't be too sure of it. My hunch says they're off to give Mulehead Valley the once-over.' He straightened his hat and gave his belt a hitch. 'I'll get my horse and follow them. I'm real keen to know what those gents are up to.'

'Then I'd better go with you.'

'No need to, Hab. Besides, they might get wise to two *hombres* riding on their back trail. I'll make sure they don't spot me.'

Johnny went to the livery and took out his bay gelding. While he saddled, Ben Shaw talked of the two strangers riding off together. The stableman had formed the opinion that Post and Bannon were a couple of longriders on the run.

'You didn't catch where they were heading, Ben?'

'They talked in whispers, and that's what makes me think they're up to no good. I did hear the thin gent say something about a ranch.'

70

'A ranch, huh? Thanks, pard.'

Johnny rode out of town at an easy canter, but once clear of the last huddle of buildings he raised the gelding's pace to a run, veering to the south-west and the direction of Mulehead Valley. He revelled in the feel of a good horse under him, the sage-scented wind against his cheeks, the sense of freedom he experienced when he took to horseback.

Buying the old Benson place might not be such a bad idea, he reflected. True, he would have to work harder than he had ever worked in his life. But he believed it was a goal well worth achieving. Then he would have something worthwhile to offer Ginny Ford in the event of . . .

'Easy, you loco gazebo,' he chided himself with a laugh. 'Ginny hasn't said she'll marry you, so you'd better not jump fences until you come to them.'

The country he travelled was fairly rough for the first few miles, and then he crested a low, grassed ridge where there were small parks choked with wild flowers. So far he had not seen any sign of the men ahead of him, but he spotted enough tracks to tell him that Bannon and Post really were making a beeline for Mulehead Valley. They would have obtained precise directions from someone before leaving town and should find the place easily enough.

Topping out a hill, Johnny saw two riders in front of him and perhaps a mile distant. They took a trail that skirted a stretch of woodland and soon went from his view. Drawing close to the timbered ridges that provided the best access to the valley from this side, he made a short detour that took him in among the rock walls flanking the west side of the valley. A stranger riding through here would be surprised to discover pretty good cow country on the other side of those walls.

He left the gelding in a cluster of boulders where a fissure drove through the cliffs, and entered the valley below the actual ranch site. Ten minutes later he was at the base of a huge sandstone rock where he was afforded a reasonably good view of the tumble-down ranch buildings. He saw Fred Post and Luke Bannon sitting their saddles in the front yard and opposite the sagging porch. There was a veritable jungle of weeds over yonder, and the warm breeze carried a cloying sweetness.

Post and his companion appeared to be discussing some aspect of the place. They were smoking, and the thin man kept gesturing to various features that claimed his attention. They dismounted at length and stood looking around them before going on to the house. They remained inside for only a few minutes, and when they emerged they shifted across to the clutter of out-houses.

Johnny was so engrossed that the faint scuffle behind him took a second to register. Alarmed, he grabbed for the six-shooter at his hip, but before he could complete his draw something hard caught him on the back of the neck and sent him sprawling to the ground with his senses churning into a crazy maelstrom.

5

He came to with an agonising pain in his head and at the base of his neck. The pain flowed through his shoulders and into his arms. Yet, when he moved slightly it withdrew mercifully from his arms and concentrated on the walls of his skull. He opened his eyes to the burnished mirror of the sky, eased himself to his knees and stood up. As soon as he did so he threatened to lose balance. He clawed at the edge of a boulder for support and held on until the grogginess receded.

Next, he explored the area of his head where that heavy blow had connected. There was a sizeable bump and a thin crusting of dried blood. Then he remembered the scuffling in the shale and brought his gun from its holster. There was nothing behind him now, of course. Whoever had sneaked up on him and slugged him had made himself scarce.

'Who?' he snarled bitterly, looking towards the ranch house where he had last seen Lute Bannon and Fred Post. There was no sign of the men nor of their horses. It could not have been either of the hardcases who had crawled through the rocks and inflicted the injury. Which meant there must have been a third man somewhere, watching him and waiting for the right moment to strike.

He retraced his steps to the spot where he had left the bay and led the horse to the open. He left it again with reins trailing while, Colt at the ready, he investigated the main building and then each of the outhouses. He was returning to the front yard when he heard approaching hoofbeats. He hurried to his bay and took it to the gable where it would not be seen immediately by the oncoming rider. Then he crouched and waited, wincing against the pain that plagued his neck and shoulders.

He swore when he recognised Ray Glover, mounted on a rented chestnut. The land agent continued slowly until he reached the front of the building, where he halted and froze as Johnny stepped out of cover, revolver levelled.

'It's you, Carver . . . ' Glover choked at length after a fear-charged pause. Then, with anger taking over: 'What's going on here?'

'I might ask you the same thing, Mr Glover.' It seemed inconceivable that Glover had been his assailant, but in a situation like this anything was possible.

'What!' the land agent exclaimed. 'What are you talking about — say, you look as if you've been hurt,' he added when Johnny appeared to stagger.

'I'm improving,' Johnny said drily. 'But I wasn't in good trim a little while back.'

'What happened?' Glover demanded, sliding from his saddle. 'And put that damn gun away, if you please, sir.'

Johnny hesitated, his gaze running over him. The land agent wore no weapon that was visible, nor did he carry a saddle-gun. Still, he could have a pistol hidden in the folds of that clawhammer coat. He looked cool enough where another man might be sweating in the torrid heat.

Johnny shrugged finally and pouched his Colt. The idea of Ray Glover being his attacker was just too silly to consider.

'I had an accident of sorts,' he explained. 'A mishap, you might call it. Did you meet anybody on your way out here?'

Glover shook his head. He seemed genuinely puzzled. There actually was a sheen of sweat on his forehead. His eyes narrowed at the way the deputy kept lifting his shoulders and wincing.

'What sort of mishap? It strikes me that whatever happened must have muddled your thinking.'

'I guess so.' The wariness returned to Johnny's eyes. 'You're sure you met nobody on the trail?'

'I said so,' was the testy response.

'Who do you imagine I might have met?'

'Well, that Fred Post gent, for a start. He came here with his pard that we had in jail. I was tracking them to see what they'd get up to. I detoured and came into the valley through the rocks back yonder. I was watching them when some sidewinder happened along and nearly cracked my skull.'

'Hell no!' Glover gulped, staring anxiously around him. 'You don't suppose that Post is a — '

'Crook?' Johnny suggested. 'I don't have all the answers I need yet. Look, Mr Glover, now that you're here, could I put something to you?'

The land agent paused so that he might frame his words carefully. 'I suppose that would depend on what you're talking about.'

'I'm talking about this layout,' Johnny explained, touching the back of his neck gingerly. 'You said that if I decided to buy the Benson place I could have it. Right?'

'The first person to be granted the deeds — not immediately, I might say — will be the lawful owner.' He relented to the extent of smiling. 'You're not seriously considering buying it yourself?'

'Why not?' Johnny countered. 'Mr Glover, you've been around Stockwell as long as anybody. You've got as big a stake in the town as anyone can claim. I just don't think it would be a good idea if that bird Post got control of this place.'

'That has occurred to me,' Glover murmured. He reached a decision. 'Do you really intend buying this layout, Johnny?'

'If we can come to an agreement on terms.'

'Right. Then let's get back to town. Under the circumstances, the sooner you take title the better. First come, first served.'

Before quitting the valley by the main entrance, Johnny back-tracked to the rocks and the gap where he had come through. He spent a while searching but gave up at length. His attacker, whoever he was, had made himself scarce. 'I just hope he shows his hand again,' he mused.

The land agent had waited for him and they rode out of the canyon together, taking the overgrown track that bent to the north-east and which would pick up one of the many trails leading to town. Johnny kept scanning the country on all sides but he saw nothing out of the ordinary. If someone had followed him out of town to see what he was up to, he might still be around somewhere.

They arrived in Stockwell without incident and he told Ray Glover he would call at his office as soon as he had reported to the sheriff. Glover cast an uneasy eye along the busy main street.

'Don't wait too long,' he advised. 'If Post gets to me first there's not a damned thing I can do about it. Remember what I said. First come, first

served must remain my motto. Otherwise my reputation would suffer.'

'I get the drift,' Johnny said drily.
'Don't worry. I'll be there before you
can take your hat off.'

He racked his bay at the rail fronting
the law office and went inside. Buck
Arden was in charge.

'Hab left a few minutes ago,' the
jailer explained. 'Said he was going to
buy tobacco for his pipe. Say,' he added
concernedly, 'you don't look so good.
Anything the matter?'

'I'll tell you about it later.' Johnny
swung back to the street. He spotted
Hab Beely on his way out of Jud
Wayne's store. Hab was filling his pipe
from a new pack of rough-cut. His eyes
glinted at sight of his deputy.

'You're back, I see . . . What in hell's
wrong with you? You didn't have
another run-in with those gents?'

Johnny took him to a corner where
there was little likelihood of anyone
overhearing what they said, and when
he related what had happened at

Mulehead Valley, Beely swore forcefully.

'Somebody snuck up through the rocks and let you have it on the skull? But who was it if it wasn't Post or Bannon?'

'Wish I knew, Hab. I've been racking my brains for the answer. No use thinking it was Ray Glover, because Glover wouldn't have the nerve even if he did want to soften my skull a mite.'

'But it just has to be linked to those *hombres*, boy. I know it in my bones. They caught on you were following them and had this third gent lie up and knock you senseless.'

'But why? Why knock me out because I was having a look-see?'

'Sounds strange, I grant,' the sheriff nodded. 'Anyhow, we'll have to — '

He broke off, wheeling at the sound of hoofbeats coming into town from the west end of Main. Johnny Carver soon chuckled grimly.

'Another stranger, Hab.'

'Sure as the devil! Got the same cut as the other two . . . '

The man they referred to was mounted on a scraggy-looking buckskin. He was of medium build, dark and bearded, and when he drew closer they saw that he packed two revolvers in low-slung holsters. As he progressed along the dusty street his eyes kept shifting this way and that. They rested on the two lawmen for the space of a second, skidded on over them as if he considered them of small importance. He continued to the hitchrack at the front of Saul Darton's saloon, where he dismounted.

Hab Beely rubbed his jaw. 'I guess I must be going crazy, boy.'

'Not so you'd notice, Hab. So now we've got a nestful of gunhawks. Lute Bannon hit town and went into Darton's to play hob with Ed Kirby. Fred Post made Darton's his first port of call. Now we've got this fella with the sharp nose and enough hardware strung around him to start a war ... Sure as heck, they arranged to come to town that way. They knew about Saul Darton's place in advance. They marked it as a meeting place, and — Hab, did you notice if Post and Bannon came back to town?'

Beely shook his head. He was watching the bearded newcomer with a sort of horrified fascination. He knew in his heart that Stockwell was about to have a change of weather. The advent of the three strangers was only the beginning. By nightfall the town would be full of them. They would be standing three-deep in the road, and that same road would be running in blood . . .

Hab shook himself. He was scared as hell, and, better still, he was ready to admit it.

The bearded stranger was on the plankwalk now, was taking a cheroot from a pocket in his scuffed, dusty vest. He trapped the tobacco stick between his teeth and scratched a match alight on the seat of his denim pants. He puffed the cheroot to life and flipped the match to the roadway. A tow-headed urchin came past. He appeared to have lost something and the stranger spoke to him. The urchin answered and the stranger delved into another pocket and produced a coin. He laughed as he spun it and the urchin caught it the way a dog catches a stick.

Now the bearded newcomer had a long look up and down the street before shouldering on through to the saloon.

Johnny Carver was moving off when the sheriff clawed at his shoulder, holding him. 'Take it easy, boy. No call to get het up.'

'You going soft in your old age, Hab? You never see that trick with a dime before . . . ?'

'Damn it, boy, you know what I mean. But you can't just brace a stranger and throw him into jail.'

'We did it with Bannon. And who mentioned jail anyhow?'

'First time they were trying to get our measure.' Beely said in a rush. 'Don't you see, boy, that could be the hellion who bounced the barrel of his gun on your head at Mulehead Valley.'

The possibility had not escaped Johnny. But quite apart from that, there was the danger of these three elements coming together explosively — Bannon, Post and the bearded newcomer. So far there was no sign of Fred Post or Lute Bannon on the street, and if he got to the newcomer straight off he might profit from the advantage of surprise.

'I'm going to have a pow-wow with him,' he told Hab. 'Maybe you should hang back and watch for the others.'

'Nix on that,' Beely growled. 'If you aim to pull that fella's beard, I want to be there when you do it.'

'Please, Hab, let me do this on my own. I've made up my mind about the Benson place in Mulehead Valley. I'm going to buy it before these birds go to roost there.'

He left the sheriff and angled for the opposite side of the street. One of these days Hab Beely would say to him, 'Just who in blazes is running this burg?' And Hab might decide to give him his marching orders. 'Which will be all right with me,' Johnny muttered. He had not gone far, however, when he heard the stout man's familiar tread behind him.

He reached the rack where the buckskin stood, went boldly to the animal and searched under the mane for a brand. Hab Beely watched him.

'Well?' Beely said in a scratchy voice.

'Nothing. Just like the others. Maybe they really did break these nags for themselves. But I still doubt it.'

He was turning from the hitchrack when the batwing doors of the saloon creaked open and the bearded man emerged. He stood, stocky legs splayed, thumbs hooked in his shell belt. A sneer made his mouth ugly.

'What's the bright idea, friend?' he demanded in a boisterous way. 'You never see something on four legs before? Maybe there's something odd about my nag that tickles your fancy?'

Johnny dragged a slow breath to his lungs. The last thing he wanted was a wordy showdown right here on the main street. But already several ears had picked up the exchange and people stopped to stare curiously.

'I can look all I want, mister,' he replied coolly. 'Do you get touchy when somebody gives your horse the once-over?'

'Touchy enough, I guess. That nag cost, although you might not believe it.' He struck a match for a cheroot, added while slanting a look at the sheriff: 'He's a nervous critter, and he don't like folks pawing over him. Even if they do happen to pack badges.'

Hab Beely slid his bulky figure between his deputy and the stranger. Hab had noticed the lumping of Johnny's jaw and the brittle light that could leap into his eye. He mustered a grin and spread his hands in a plea for tolerance.

'Hold it, folks! No call to jump in at the deep end.' He put his grin on the bearded newcomer. 'Howdy, mister. Saw you ride into town and I said to myself — '

'Hab,' Johnny interrupted in a deceptively mild tone, 'would you oblige me by taking your fat rump out of my sight.'

Beely wheeled, his face pale with angry shock. He caught his deputy's sly wink and swallowed a threatened outburst. The bearded man threw his head back and laughed. Then he thrust a forefinger at Johnny.

'Wait a minute, sonny. I reckon you should have the manners to take your turn. Dad here got his nickel's worth in first. How about it, Dad?'

'Have your say,' Beely invited in a clipped manner. 'But you'd better talk sense.'

'I'll do that, Sheriff. The name's Sime Cowley, if you want to remember it. But your deputy was going on about my horse . . . '

'It ain't branded,' Hab said in the same crisp fashion. 'Where do you hail from, mister?'

'Never took the bother to brand it. Where do I hail from? That's my

90

business and none of yours.'

He rolled himself up on his toes as he spoke, the lips curling under the beard, the eyes glinting with savage, disdainful challenge.

Johnny Carver spoke from clenched teeth. 'We'll let that ride, Cowley. Which way did you come into town? You ever hear of Mulehead Valley?'

'Mulehead Valley?' An amused chuckle. 'No, I never heard of it. Any reason I should?'

'Happens there is. If you don't know the name I bet you know where it's located. You prowled in there after me a while ago. You sneaked up on me and hit me on the head with a rock or one of your guns.'

'That a fact now?' The man's demeanour hardened even more. The narrow eyes appeared to hood. The hands came away from the gun belt and spread like poised wings above the black gun grips. 'Well, you're pushing this further than I'm willing to let you, sonny. You're trying to push me to the

limit, huh? Well, you've reached it, kid
. . . Now,' he added in a charged
whisper, 'back down pronto or make
your play!'

His right hand was clawing for the
.45 Colt in the low-slung pouch before
Johnny Carver went into action. There
was a deafening roar accompanied by a
puff of smoke and a spit of flame. The
man called Sime Cowley began rocking
slowly backwards and forwards while
amazement slackened his mouth and
crawled upwards until it touched his
eyes.

A red blob spread steadily over his
chest. The unused six-gun spilled from
his fingers and hit the planking, making
a hollow, melancholy thud. Then the
bearded stranger pitched forward and
Hab Beely's deputy was obliged to step
aside and give him space to fall.

6

There was tense silence for a moment after the man's body slammed to the boardwalk. Even Johnny Carver, the killer Colt still smoking in his fist, appeared to be frozen in the razor-sharp readiness that had stood him in such good stead.

Hab Beely was the first to approach Sime Cowley. He reached down to catch the man's shoulder and bring him around until he lay, face up. The eyes stared back at him, wide in horrified surprise. The mouth under the beard was twisted in pained bewilderment.

'Well, he's dead,' Beely grunted at length, although everyone knew the stranger was dead.

'He asked for it,' Johnny Carver said in much the same way he would have commented about the weather.

The sheriff merely nodded. He was

annoyed with his deputy for a reason he could not readily understand. It was not simply the fact that Johnny had reacted so swiftly and devastatingly to the stranger's raw challenge: Johnny had as much right as anyone to defend himself; rather, it was the cool manner with which the younger man had drawn his gun and fired that would require some time to analyse.

For a blinding instant just then, Sheriff Hab Beely had seen his deputy — not in the role of a lawman — but in that of an unfeeling killer.

A crowd was gathering and Johnny suddenly felt uncomfortable. He pushed his revolver away in its pouch as if he was not really responsible for the way it had performed. He was about to ask the sheriff what they should do with Cowley's body when a commotion broke out in the roadway behind them.

'Plain murder it was!' somebody yelped. 'He never gave the poor fool a chance . . . '

Johnny felt himself going hot and

cold in turn. The coldness was an icy chill that raced along his spine, and it took only a moment for him to spy Lute Bannon and Fred Post. They thrust through to the forefront of the gathering and halted there, dangerously defiant.

'That's a damnable lie,' Johnny mouthed angrily. Hab Beely caught his arm as he started to move forward. Hab spoke hoarsely.

'Let them be, boy. Don't let them rile you.'

Johnny shook himself free and cuffed his hat off his brow. The two strangers stood in slack-bodied stance, hands well clear of their weapons, even if they did intend using them.

'You're a liar,' Johnny repeated to Lute Bannon. 'He forced me into it. He was aiming to kill me. Turned out he was just a braggart.'

Bannon and Fred Post exchanged quick looks and then the lanky Bannon said: 'Is that so? Well, I saw it different, and I wasn't a mile away neither when it happened. The gent you bored saw you working at his nag. He said something to you, and be damned if you didn't burn him down!'

'That's another lie,' Hab Beely told the crowd milling around for better positions. 'He wants to stir more trouble, and we've got enough trouble as it is.'

'I'll say you have!' Bannon spat derisively.

The crowd split as Johnny moved over to stand directly in front of Bannon and his friend. He addressed himself to the lanky man. 'Maybe you want to take up where your pard finished?' he suggested icily.

'Pard!' Fred Post spat. 'What the devil are you talking about? That ain't no pard of ours.'

Johnny's cheeks had been pale and cold but a strong heat began to push into them. He was certain that Bannon and Post were bluffing, and that their original plan was to trim him down to size in front of the crowd. They had no intention of allowing the young deputy to make capital out of that eye-baffling fast draw and straight shot.

'He said his name was Sime Cowley,' Johnny declared and waited.

'Could be Paul Bunyan and it wouldn't make any difference to us, Deputy. We never met him, so he's no pard of ours.'

'So why do you want to stick up for him?'

'We're sticking up for the truth, mister,' Fred Post retorted loudly. 'Man with a badge ought to have more control of himself. Wouldn't you say so, Sheriff?'

'You're wasting your breath, friend,' Hab Beely grated. 'You gents are out to make trouble, and I'm sure as hell losing patience with you. Now, if you're not off the street in two minutes flat you'll find yourselves in the lock-up.'

Lute Bannon started to protest, but Fred Post caught his arm. 'What's the use?' he snorted. 'If the folks in this town want a killer for a lawman, that's their business.'

It was too much for Johnny Carver to swallow and, before Hab Beely could restrain him, he lunged at the squat man with his balled right fist swinging at his jaw. Post tried to scramble out of range, at the same time attempting to duck, but the blow thudded home and flung him on to the road on his back.

'Damn you, Deputy — '

Post snatched for the gun at his hip. There was a flurry of movement from Johnny Carver and then that Colt was aimed at the stranger's face. 'Let it be, Fred!' Johnny hissed.

Post's blunt-nosed face had gone a dirty grey shade. Sweat oozed from his brow and streamed into his jowls. If he had expected to push Johnny into a fight and get the drop on him, he had failed badly. Lute Bannon stood off a little, declaring himself neutral for the time being.

Post struggled to his feet. He stooped to recover his hat, tugged it on, and pointed a quivering forefinger at the deputy. 'I'm not through with you, friend. I promise you!'

'Let's have you right now,' was the scornful rejoinder. 'You gents are mighty big when it comes to talking. But when it comes to fighting you don't amount to shucks.'

'You'll see, mister. You'll see.'

He slouched away across the road and Lute Bannon went after him. They mounted the sidewalk, still under the watchful eye of Johnny Carver, and paused there to argue bitterly for a while before breasting the swing doors of the Cowbell saloon and going from view.

A shudder ran through Johnny Carver and he slanted a bleak smile at Hab Beely. 'It had to be done, Hab. If you let a mad dog bite you it'll come back for more and maybe chew your leg off. Say, did I do something wrong, old-timer?'

Beely had no immediate answer to make. He stooped over the dead man to search his pockets and produced a wallet that had fifty-odd dollars tucked inside. There was nothing to help determine the identity of the newcomer who had called himself Sime Cowley, much less indicate the nature of his business.

Hab Beely picked out a bystander. 'Joe, get a couple of boys and take this fella to the undertaker's place. You, Johnny,' he added with a steely inflection, 'bring the horse to the livery and tell Shaw to look after it. I'll see you in my office afterwards.'

'I'll be there, Sheriff.'

With a lingering, reluctant glance at the Cowbell, Johnny untied the buckskin's reins and led it to the livery stable. Ben Shaw was standing at the corner of the alley, attracted by the ruckus.

'That was certainly something to see,' he chuckled. 'They say the stranger was drawing when you unlimbered and let him have it.'

'I guess I beat him to it, Ben.'

'Well, I'll tell a man!' Shaw spat in the dust, became boldly mischievous. 'What's gotten into you, Johnny? That's what I'd like to know.'

'You crazy or something?' the younger man protested.

'Not so you'd notice. Look — ' Bright eyes twinkled. — 'three gents hit this burg the same day and we see more fuss than we usually see in a year. And then our quiet, gentlemanly deputy comes along, and — '

'Let it ride, Ben. Was just a stroke of luck I out-drew him.'

Shaw slapped his shoulder, chuckling harder than ever. 'That's just what it was, boy! A stroke of luck. That's what I'll tell everybody it was.' He took the buckskin horse, cackling his amusement.

Johnny dallied on a street corner where he could view the four men who lifted the body of Sime Cowley and placed it in the well of a flat-bottomed rig. A townsman scrambled to the driving seat and spun the harness horse around in the road. He cut out for the undertaker's, three blocks away.

Johnny fished for his Durham sack and rolled a smoke. He was surprised at how steady his fingers were, considering the turmoil still raging in him. He had the feeling that the showdown with Sime Cowley marked some turning point and, like it or not, he had proved something to himself.

'Proved what?' he mused bitterly. 'That I know how to drag a gun out of leather? That I know how to shoot another man dead before he shoots me?'

He studied the busy street from hooded, brooding eyes. There was no sign of the sheriff. Hab had likely gone straight to his office and was waiting there for him to show up. Poor old Hab. He had been given the surprise of his life when his deputy put his natural aptitude with a six-shooter to such use. Hab was known to frown on trick-shots and quick-draw showmen. But his deputy had gone much further than that. Hab might even fire him.

'He can please himself.'

Johnny flung his half-smoked cigarette away and cut along to the sheriff's quarters. Hab was seated behind his desk, chin cupped in his hands. A cloud of worry serrated his brow. Of Buck Arden there was no sign.

Johnny decided to take the bull by the horns. 'What happens now?' he demanded flatly. 'Do you want me to quit?'

Beely raised his head and regarded him for a moment without speaking. He touched his lips with the tip of his tongue and mustered a wry grin. 'What happens?' he echoed. 'I'm supposed to know that? How in hell do I know? I feel like the sky might fall down any minute. You heard that gent Post. He's mean and ornery. Which just begins to describe that rat-eyed Bannon.'

Johnny cleared his throat. 'It's easy to see they were in with Cowley. I'm pretty sure it was Cowley who slugged me out at Mulehead Valley. But I didn't want to kill him, Hab. I really didn't.'

'I know.' Beely lifted his heavy shoulders, let them sag. His smile was touched with whimsy. 'A gent is sometimes forced into doing something he'd rather not do. No, I don't blame you, Johnny. There was a time when I'd have chawed Cowley whole and spit out his bones. Maybe I've gone soft and didn't know it.'

'You're blaming yourself for hiring me, for pinning this badge to my shirt? You'd like to wipe the slate clean as far as I'm concerned?'

'What in blue blazes are you talking about?' Beely rounded on him. 'Are you getting cold feet after the big show?'

'I'm thinking about you. You might have handled it differently. You'd have talked with Cowley, got him to simmer down. But I killed him, and now his pards will want to take it out on both of us.'

'You really believe he was in with those two jaspers?'

'I'm sure of it. I'll tell you something

else I'm sure of,' Johnny added with a ring in his voice. 'We'll soon see more of them. A dozen. Maybe a score. Yeah, I mean it, Hab! You'll soon see more strangers riding down that street. There's something real bad in the air. That means there could be a hell of a fight. And if they want a fight we'll have to be ready to oblige. Now, if you're not prepared to do that, you'd better have my badge right now.'

Hab Beely half-rose from his chair, his mouth hardening to a white, lumpish line. He hauled a long, shuddering breath to his lungs, then subsided, swallowing the torrent he had been about to spew forth. He resumed his seat and drew his palms across his face. He produced his pipe with a great display of deliberation and caught it between his teeth, threatening to snap the stem.

'You got a match?' he said when the tension eased in him.

'Sure thing, Hab.'

Johnny struck a match and handed it over. He made a hasty exit from the office and stood on the plankwalk, squinting into the brittle afternoon sunshine. After a few minutes he gave his belt a hitch and angled across the road, heading for the false-fronted building with the fading painting of a cowbell above the doorway. He was only mildly disappointed to discover that Lute Bannon and Fred Post had gone. It had been his intention to issue a final and uncompromising warning to the strangers: if they took so much as a single step out of line he would tell them to leave town and not dare to even look back.

A little of the steam ran out of him as he stood, just inside the batwings, eyeing the half-dozen patrons at the bar and the three loafers playing cards for dimes. Hal Fletcher, the bartender, glanced in his direction and looked away uneasily.

'Howdy, Johnny,' he greeted in a bluff manner. 'Looking for somebody?'

'Two drifters, Hal. They came in here.'

'Sure, they did. They had a couple of drinks and left.'

Johnny nodded. Normally these patrons of the Cowbell would have been easy and friendly and would have drawn him into conversation about something or other. But he had out-drawn Sime Cowley — an unknown quantity, to be sure — but even so, the deputy's coolness and the speed of his draw had altered his status in a way that meant he could never revert to being the Johnny Carver they had always known.

The notion had a profoundly sobering effect on Johnny. He spent thirty minutes patrolling the town's main street, but saw no sign of Bannon or his sidekick. Then the obvious tack occurred to him and he bent his steps towards the livery stable, where he learned that Bannon and Post had not put their horses up since leaving town earlier. It meant that, on returning from Mulehead Valley, they must have left their horses in an alley or side street. So it must be assumed they had ridden out.

Now Johnny remembered he had promised to turn up at Ray Glover's office to settle the deal for the old Benson ranch. He hurried to the land office and was ushered through to Glover's sanctum.

The land agent's frown told its own story, as did the tight smile that puckered his lips. He gestured to the chair opposite his desk.

'Heard you had more bother since I left you, Johnny. You said you'd — '

'I couldn't make it,' Johnny was aware of a lurching sensation in the pit of his stomach. 'If you've heard about the bother you must know what kept me.'

'You're too late,' the other informed him with an exaggerated grimace. 'Yes, you are, Johnny. Fred Post was here a while ago. He said he'd had a look at Mulehead. He figures he can make a go of it. He paid a twenty per cent deposit and promised to meet the balance before the week's out.'

'Well, hell!' Johnny exploded. 'So you

let him beat me to it? You knew I was going to buy the ranch. You knew Post was a stranger and we didn't want him getting his hands on the valley . . . '

The land agent's jaw lumped. A glint of anger sharpened his gaze. He raised a hand in protest. 'I think you'd better get this straight, Deputy. I laid it on the line for you. I've got a reputation for fair play and I aim to keep it. You had your chance, the same as Post had. If you really wanted that spread you should have clinched the deal before the stranger came along.'

'But damn it, Ray, I didn't know — Oh, forget it,' he grated in disgust. 'So long as you got your payoff you're happy. But I'm going to tell you something you'd better chew over hard, mister: before those gents pull out of this territory you might regret what you've done.'

Glover would have continued trying to justify his action, but Johnny was already on the way out. He slammed the door hard on his heels and ploughed on to the street. There, he paused to calm himself, but it was difficult being calm in the circumstances. Lawyers and land agents, he thought savagely, they were a blight on any community. But the damage was done and there was nothing he could do to remedy it.

Hab Beely was in the doorway of the law office when he arrived there, and the sheriff knew by the thunderous look on the younger man's face that something was badly amiss.

'What's eating you?' he demanded anxiously. 'Seems that pair have left town.'

'They've left all right,' Johnny snorted. 'Would you like to make a guess where they're headed?'

Beely was in no mood for guessing games and he said so. Then he had an inspiration. 'You're not saying that Glover sold them the Mulehead Valley ranch?'

'That's exactly what he did, Hab. I told him I aimed to buy it to keep them

110

from getting it. But Mr Glover is a stickler for fair play and his own brand of ethics. But believe me, sir, his ethics are going to choke him one of these days.'

'So those hellions actually own Mulehead Valley?' Beely croaked as the full implication registered.

'As good as, Hab. Glover let Fred Post settle the deal behind my back. And that proves those birds are not just drifters stopping off on their way through this neck of the woods. They're here to stay, and they must have a damned good reason for taking over the Benson ranch.'

'Well curse Glover anyhow!' Beely stormed. 'If I thought he was trying to put one over on us . . . ' He let the rest trickle off. Then, in a ragged whisper: 'Look what the wind's blowing in now, boy.'

Johnny turned to look along the main street. Four horsemen had entered from the west end of town. They were spread out and riding at a leisurely pace while they glanced this way and that, taking in everything, occasionally exchanging observations. There was no doubt that they were total strangers to the territory, and for a split second Johnny Carver knew a lancing of fear that threatened to paralyse him.

'More trouble, Hab,' he breathed. 'And I'll bet my boots they belong to the same outfit as Post and Bannon.'

7

For Hab Beely it was one of the worst moments in his career. It was like having an old, recurrent nightmare finally manifest itself as a reality. The peaceful days in Stockwell were over and these newcomers heralded the beginnings of a new and sinister phase in the town's history.

It did not occur to Hab that they might simply be drifting riders who planned to stop off for a meal and a drink on their way to whatever destination they had in mind. Yesterday, he would have been willing to compromise with his burgeoning anxiety, but today was different. That lanky, cross-eyed Lute Bannon had set the pattern; Fred Post had traced his way into it, and the stranger Sime Cowley who had died at the end of Johnny Carver's flaming six-gun had been part of it also.

These four strangers chopping through the sun-silvered dust merely emphasised the menacing overtones.

'What do we do now, Hab?'

It was a question of his own thrown back at him. Whatever Johnny Carver had proved himself to be, he would be no match for these travel-stained, bleak-featured hardcases. For a split second, Hab longed to be far away from here, riding clear and free, with the weight of the badge he carried unlimbered along the way.

Then, as suddenly as the feeling had touched him, the terror vanished and the anxiety became a slow, unhurried rhythm instead of a hard, insistent throbbing. He recalled a day when he had been deputy sheriff under Ezra Blaidsall. He was young then and bursting with a frenzied get-up-and-go energy. A report had reached town about a shooting over at Riley's Ford.

'You go over there, Hab, and look into it,' Blaidsall had ordered him. 'Do what you can but don't get them high tail-feathers chopped off by lead. A man behaving too damn prideful and foolish is liable to end up with a mouthful of dust.'

Beely remembered those words. They could hardly have been called samples of the most profound wisdom, but they had stuck in his mind.

The young deputy had collected his pony from the livery barn and set off on the trail to the small township. The raw courage flowed freely in his veins as he arrived in Riley's Ford and met the town marshal. According to the marshal, a gunman was holed up in the Dollar saloon. He had already wounded two people, and he might wound — or kill — more unless somebody got close enough to take his gun from him.

The town marshal offered to accompany the vinegary Hab to the Dollar, but Ezra Blaidsall's deputy allowed that he would rather try and settle the issue on his own. And, true to his nature in those heady days, he forgot everything that Blaidsall had drummed into him.

He had headed along to the saloon, where he was greeted with a wild yell on his arrival at the swing-doors bearing the large dollar signs. The crazy character in there said he would shoot the first mother's son to put his nose inside the batwings. And then, horror of horrors, the thought of being shot to death became so vivid that the young deputy's courage melted like snow in warm sunlight. For a sickening moment there was a gap where his stomach should rightly be, and his legs appeared to have forgotten how to keep his body upright.

A bullet blasting from the depths of the saloon had restored his equilibrium. The slug raged over Hab's head, missing him by scant inches. And suddenly a strange, new-found fury welled up in him that swamped out every other consideration, so that, before he actually knew what he was doing, he shouldered straight into the saloon and right up to the tawny-haired *hombre* standing by the bar with an old

Remington in his hand.

'Give me that, you ugly bastard,' Hab ordered the blackguard.

'I'm gonna kill you,' the other chattered and lifted the gun.

Hab saw something not too far back in the fellow's eye that gave him his cue for the ensuing proceedings. 'You don't have the guts to kill a bug,' he informed the villain. 'Now, hand me that iron or I'll tear your arms off and beat the brains out of your fool head.'

The man promptly broke down and blubbered, and Hab soon had the Remington in his possession. The town marshal showed up and Hab told him to bring irons and a horse that wouldn't shy away from something that was all yellow. By sundown the badman was behind bars in Stockwell. The town marshal accompanied Hab there and, in spite of Hab's protestations, commended his bravery to the sheriff.

'I knew you were a brave man,' Ezra Blaidsall complimented him later. Blaidsall had his tongue in his cheek, but he actually meant every word that he said. Hab, however, just grinned and shook his head.

'Believe me, Sheriff, I wasn't acting brave. Truth is, I was acting like a damn fool.'

'*Just a damn fool . . .* '

'Come again,' Johnny Carver said as he glanced curiously at the sheriff. 'You starting to talk to yourself, old man?'

'I'm not an old man, and don't call me one.'

'Well, anyhow . . . what do we do now?' Johnny was watching the four strangers again. 'They're stopping outside the Cottonwood. No, they're not! They're coming on. Say, if they see us standing here with our mouths open they might get the idea — '

'Let them think what they want,' Hab Beely growled.

The horsemen drew closer, drew level. They were rangy, grim-featured men, roughly clad, gun-hung. They forked lean, shaggy, trail-tired horses. One of the men was sallow-faced and sported a pitiful moustache. He was riding a dun with white stockings on its forelegs. He eyed the two lawmen and raised a gloved hand in grudging salute. That was all. Then they were past and turning in at the front of Saul Darton's saloon. They took their time over racking their mounts and clumping over the planking with much fuss and spur-jangling. Before entering the saloon each of them turned to take another look at the watching lawmen.

'Whew!' Johnny spat in the dust and rubbed the angle of his jaw. Hab Beely fished his pipe out and got his tobacco pouch. His fingers were steady enough. Johnny was peeling away when the sheriff spoke roughly.

'You take it easy, mister. Let them set for a while. Worst thing you can do is act like you're scared of them.'

'Are you scared, Hab?'

'Just a little,' the stout man replied in a measured fashion. 'But maybe you ain't?'

'I reckon I'm a bit nervous,' Johnny

admitted with a wry grin. 'But remember, Hab, if they're pards of that Sime Cowley and the other two, they might act up when they hear I drilled Cowley.'

'I still say we ought to wait and see,' Beely said conclusively and continued tamping tobacco into the bowl of his pipe.

★   ★   ★

The afternoon waned and the four strangers remained in Saul Darton's saloon. At dusk, John Evans came to the law office to complain about Hank Bryson. Bryson was a town loafer who occasionally managed to get his hands on a bottle of cheap liquor, and when he did he was wont to stir up trouble.

'Where's Hank at now, Mr Evans?' Johnny had eaten supper at Ma Pearson's cafe and was holding down the office until Sheriff Beely had his meal. There was no way of knowing what kind of night it would be or how long it would last.

'Bryson claims he wants to buy shells for a Greener shotgun, Johnny. He knows well enough I don't stock guns and shells. I sent him to Pauley's place, but he says I'm a liar and don't want to serve him.'

'Where's Hank at, Mr Evans?'

'Why, hell, at my store.'

'Oh, he is, is he?' Buck Arden had dropped by to see if he would be needed tonight. As well as functioning as jailer, Arden often filled in for extra duties, for which he was paid a little more.

'No, I'll go, Buck,' Johnny told the elderly man. 'You stay here till Hab gets back. Let's go to your store and settle this, Mr Evans.'

John Evans had his hardware store on Dixon Avenue, a side artery forking off Main. On their arrival the store was empty apart from Evans' clerk who was impatient to close up and be off home, and Hank Bryson who was seated on a nail keg, empty bottle in hand, a bemused look in his watery eyes.

'What's to do, Hank?' Johnny demanded gruffly. 'What's this about wanting shotgun shells? When did you get your hands on a Greener?'

'Me, Johnny?' Bryson drawled in a slurred voice. 'Hell, I don't own a gun. I just happened to say to John . . . '

'I know. John told me. Well, you listen to me, Hank. One more complaint about your behaviour and you go out of town on a rail. Get it, mister, a rail?'

Bryson had to be helped from the store, and Johnny took him to the opposite side of the street where a solitary sycamore grew and let him ease down into the cool shadows. Then he appropriated the bottle and flung it into a trash heap.

'Remember, Hank, I'm being easy with you this time. But if you step out of line again, Hab's going to throw the vagrancy law at you.'

'Sure, Johnny, I know. You're a good boy, Johnny. But why did Evans tell a lie?'

Johnny shrugged, a tight smile at his

mouth. He left the drunk and headed for the intersection. He had wanted to keep Darton's saloon under more or less constant surveillance until the four strangers left. He was almost at the corner when a revolver shot rang out and, immediately afterwards there was a hard flurry of hoofbeats thundering down Main towards the western outlet.

Johnny broke into a run, his stride stiff and awkward in his high-heeled boots. Rider's boots were not made for running. But for that matter, a rider was not made for running, so that, by the time he reached the corner, the galloping hoofbeats were dwindling beyond the town's outskirts.

A small crowd had gathered in the vicinity of the law office and Hab Beely was in the middle of it. Johnny breathed easier when he saw the sheriff was in one piece. Hab was swearing luridly.

'What's going on? What's all the fuss about?'

'Damned if I rightly know,' the stout man confessed. 'I was finishing supper when I heard the shot. I left Ma's and saw those jaspers riding out. It must have been one of them.'

'It was one of them right enough, Sheriff,' a bystander confirmed. 'I seen them. They came out of Darton's and mounted their nags. They were talking and laughing. Then one of them pulled his iron and shot at the sky.'

'Blazes!' Hab Beely growled. 'What do you reckon, Johnny? Suppose they heard about Cowley getting bored?'

'I don't know.' Johnny's eyes glinted in the gathering shadows. 'But it's one way of showing their defiance, I guess. Might be the last we'll see or hear of them,' he added for the benefit of the listeners rather than to convince the sheriff or himself.

'I doubt it,' Beely breathed close to his ear. 'It all fits, boy. They're off to see Post and that squint-eyed *hombre*. Now why in the name of anything did Ray Glover sell them that ranch?'

'You know that Glover would sell his mother for twenty dollars.' Johnny left the sheriff, veering to where Ed Kirby, in hat and coat, was in the process of quitting his job at Darton's for the day. Kirby would have ducked past the deputy had Johnny not grabbed his arm.

'Did you see their play, Ed?'

'The shooting?' the bartender challenged with a scowl. 'No, I didn't.' He looked pale and there were lines of strain about his eyes and mouth. 'I just heard the shot when they left. Didn't you know they were in there, drinking?' he added reproachfully.

'I was keeping an eye peeled. They didn't make trouble in the saloon?'

'No, they didn't.' Kirby wiped his face with a handkerchief. He had a bottle tucked under his left arm. He gulped a breath. 'But I could tell what they were as soon as they came in, Johnny. I was waiting for you or Hab to show up.'

'Do you know if they heard about Cowley getting bored?'

Kirby bit his underlip and nodded.

He looked guilty about something. 'They asked me if any other strangers had hit town lately. It was the one with the moustache who did the talking. He looked like he might have lung trouble. I heard them call him Mike. They bought a drink for Ted Brinkley, and I reckon they wanted to prime him.'

'Brinkley still in there?'

'Playing cards when I left. No, there he is,' Kirby corrected himself, spotting the subject of their talk in the crowd that was breaking up.

'What did you tell the bird called Mike?' Johnny asked Kirby.

'He asked me about the man you shot, Johnny. He wanted to know his name and I said I'd heard him called Cowley. What else could I say?'

'Nothing much, Ed. Don't be tough on yourself. So you figure they knew Cowley? Did they mention the other two strangers by name?'

Ed Kirby shook his head. He looked relieved now. 'It was this Mike who did the talking. Yes, I'd say they knew

126

Cowley. Strikes me they're all part of the same bunch.'

Johnny saw Ted Brinkley shuffling off into the darkness and collared him. Brinkley was a lumberyard labourer who worked hard and drank hard. Johnny recoiled from the heavy liquor smell.

'Excuse me, Ted. Heard you were drinking with these strangers. I'd like to know what they said.'

'Sure, Johnny. They asked about three other fellas they expected to meet in town. Then they asked about the one that drew on you.'

A nerve twitched at the corner of Johnny's mouth. 'You made it plain who drew first, I hope?'

'Well, I didn't see the fight, did I?' Brinkley made a careless gesture. 'But them gents know they can't walk over you, Johnny. I can tell you that.'

'Call me Deputy.'

'All right, all right! Deputy? Hell, I've always called you Johnny. Anyway, they didn't swallow that their pard had opened the ball. They seemed to think he was some shucks with his hogleg. They called me a liar when I said he drew first. I don't reckon they believe it yet.'

Johnny relented and slapped his shoulder. He told Brinkley to watch how he went. He discovered Hab Beely with three or four men whom he recognised in the gloom as members of the town council. Big Vic Buell was asking for an assurance that law and order would be upheld, no matter what.

'I'll do what I can,' the sheriff told them. 'I can't do more.'

'Course not, Hab. But we've a quiet town here and it's got to stay that way . . . Oh, hello, Johnny. There's something we'd like to take up with you pretty soon.'

'Any time you like, Mr Buell,' Johnny said unyieldingly.

The others refused to meet the deputy's narrowed, challenging eyes and the group faded off into the darkness. Johnny turned to see Hab regarding him with a thin smile at his lips.

'What's the joke, Hab?'

'No joke. Can't you see that those good men and true are shivering in their oversize boots? They want to make sure I'll hold their hand if they really get scared. You hear much from Kirby?'

Johnny related what the bartender had told him. Then he explained about his chat with Ted Brinkley. 'So there doesn't appear to be much doubt that they're all out of the one pickle barrel,' he ended grimly.

'Did you watch them ride out?' Beely asked next.

'Hank Bryson was up to his tricks again. John Evans said he was plaguing him in his store, so I sloped off to deal with Bryson. Meant I missed that gazebo trying to drill a hole in the moon.'

'I'll kick Hank Bryson's backside,' the sheriff declared. 'But what about these birds, Johnny?'

'I'd say they're headed for Mulehead

Valley. But we'll never see the day they buy a starter herd and go into proper ranching . . . I feel like strangling that damned Glover.'

'Forget it. If it wasn't the Benson place, it'd be a hole in the rocks some place else. Still, I'd like to be sure they're making for Mulehead.' He gave his nose a rub and slapped the gun at his hip. 'What say we mosey thataway and sniff around?'

There would be little profit to be gained from such a manoeuvre in the dark, Johnny thought, and said as much. 'Maybe we should let it sit until daylight. And it wouldn't be wise to go there together. From now on, one of us had better stick around town until we discover the kind of game they're playing.'

'Maybe you're right,' Hab Beely agreed, glad that he had made the proposal but pleased that Johnny had turned it down.

* ★ ★

130

It was late when Johnny went to his room at Mason's hotel. Hab had his own living quarters at the rear of his office, so that he was always on the spot if anything untoward happened. Johnny's room overlooked the main street and he sat in the musky shadows for a while, sucking at a cigarette and wondering if the four newcomers would return to town, seeking revenge for the killing of their friend.

Oddly, he was not as frightened as he might have been. He had long since accepted his facility with a six-shooter but he was still surprised at the way he had outdrawn Sime Cowley. The smooth handle of the Colt appeared to have leaped to the palm of his hand of its own volition; the index finger had gone through the guard and encircled the trigger to the mere pulse of a thought. There had been a familiar comforting sensation in the hard bucking of the revolver stock. It had only been when Cowley rocked off balance, dead on his feet, that the true horror registered. For the first time he had been dragged into a fight where he had been obliged to kill or be killed.

A tremor shook him as he relived the moment, but he shrugged it off. He closed the window shades and struck a match for the coal oil lamp bracketed on the wall above the small mirror and the washstand. He stripped to the waist, poured water from the pitcher that was filled each morning, and lathered himself with soap. He dried quickly and donned his undershirt.

Next, he sat on the edge of the made-up bed and brought his .45 from its sheath. There were four live shells in the cylinder and a spent one. He punched the spent shell out and held it between finger and thumb. A feeling akin to exhilaration took hold of him, but he quelled it, recognising the danger of earning the reputation of a gunfighter. Such a reputation served as a magnet to other gunslingers eager to enhance their questionable fame. And it might have been nothing more than a lucky shot. A fluke draw and a fluke shot. Were he ever called on to repeat the performance the cards could fall the other way, and he might be the one who turned his toes up.

Despite the soberness these reflections laid on him he buckled the gunbelt around his waist again. He looked at the shaded window and let imagination paint an enemy there. A picture of Sime Cowley rose before him. He saw the mouth twisting mockingly under the black beard, the eyes glinting, heard the brash challenge ringing out.

'*Back down pronto or make your play!*'

Johnny's fingers streaked to the butt of his Colt. It was as if the weapon leaped out of the worn leather to his hand. He aimed the gun at the window shade; his trigger finger curled and tightened. Only at the last second did he ease the pressure that would have sent a slug raging through the glass.

'You damned fool!' he berated

himself. 'You nearly let go then. There'd have been a riot and by dawn they'd be calling you crazy . . . '

Kill crazy.

He pouched the weapon, crossed to the mirror above the washstand and studied his eyes for a moment. There was no difference there. It was the same face looking out at him that greeted him while he shaved in the mornings. He tried telling himself so, but it was wrong and he was a liar. A dim flare in the pupils betrayed the trailing remnants of that moment of triumph. He even experienced a surge of eagerness when he thought of those strangers out at Mulehead Valley.

The fact was, he would never be the same Johnny Carver again.

He hung his gunbelt on the knob of the bed, pulled off boots and pants and rolled in. Then he lay, staring at the ceiling, painting his secret pictures and wondering what might become of him.

He slept at last and dreamed of Ginny Ford.

8

Johnny awoke with false dawn stirring in the east. He dressed and left the hotel without waiting for breakfast. The night man at the livery stable was sound asleep in his small, box-like office at the far end of the stable. Johnny took his bay out and saddled up without disturbing the old-timer. On Main, he cut along for the law office. The street was bare and silent; it even looked reasonably clean. Even so, unsavoury smells persisted in alleys that ended in open lots where trash was dumped for the sake of convenience.

Buck Arden had passed the night in the law office, and the outer door was drawn to but left unlocked. Buck was lying back in the desk chair, down-at-heel boots pinning the open checker board to the desk-top. The jailer rubbed his eyes and grinned sheepishly.

'Hello, Johnny. Too tired to walk to my lodgings last night . . . was this morning, really. Hab and me played checkers for hours. You ever notice how he likes to play checkers when he's worried?'

'Never paid much attention. I bet you can play in your sleep by now. Is Hab abed?'

'Sure thing. I'll go get him if you want.'

'No, let him be. I felt restless and figured I'd take an early ride.'

The jailer discarded his slow, tolerant humour. 'Johnny, you ain't going to Mulehead alone? Hab told me how that stranger bought the valley from under your nose. They say a whole lot about that old Benson place. Fit for nothing but a family of gophers. But a young fella with the right amount of ginger could get it humming in a couple of seasons.'

'Fred Post clinched the deal anyhow,' Johnny said with a shrug. 'But we can't fault Glover for selling. He's got to make a living.'

'Who're you fooling, youngster? That miser must have a fortune stashed away. And a man who's made so much out of this town should have spared a thought for its welfare.' Buck lifted his boots from the desk and struggled to his feet. He stretched and yawned. 'Say, I'll get the stove burning and fix a mug of Arbuckle. Never rightly awake till I get my mug of coffee in the mornings. Wait and join me, then I'll ride out with you.'

'No, you won't, Buck. I just want to find out what's going on at Mulehead Valley. You can bet I won't go calling at the ranch-house. I just dropped by to see if the night was quiet.'

'Oh, it was quiet enough. Say, you'd never believe it: Hank Bryson turned up to apologise for making trouble for you. Hank was a regular gent until he fell in love with a whisky bottle. You can't find the heart to kick him out of town, which is where he belongs.'

'I guess not. Well, I'll go sniff the morning breeze. Never mind telling

Hab until he gets up.'

The jailer nodded and watched him go out. He frowned thoughtfully, listening as Johnny mounted and went along the street.

Full dawn was flaring in the east now, painting the sky crimson and pearl and gold. There was a fair amount of mist hanging in the air, and the bunchgrass was liberally dusted with dew-like sparkle.

Johnny breathed deeply of the clean, cool fragrance. He had always revelled in morning rides. He enjoyed the early scent of sage and timber, reminding him as it did of the few years he had spent as a forty-a-month cowpuncher. Cowboys might complain about their lot, curse the bad grub they had to eat and the recalcitrant cattle they had to herd, but there was no way of life to equal it, in his estimation. He would cheerfully shed his deputy's badge at the drop of a hat and sign on again with one of the Morgan County ranchers.

Which brought his thoughts to Sam

Ford and his daughter, Ginny. He had known Ginny since she was no higher than a pony's belly. She was eighteen now and he was twenty-three. They had gotten along well from the very beginning. Johnny had come to this range as a fifteen-year-old orphan. His first job had been that of stable hand on Earl Patton's Lazy P spread. He had taken to Patton and his foreman, and they had always given him a fair do.

His first encounter with Ginny had occurred one day when he was a fully-fledged cowhand and riding range close to Sam Ford's territory, in search of strays. This slip of a girl had appeared from a section of brush, straddling a mount that was much too big for her. The horse had taken the bit in its teeth and made the girl's saddle a veritable hurricane deck. Johnny went after the runaway and caught it. He had scolded Ginny and she had cried bitterly. It transpired that she had taken the big grulla out without her father's permission. She begged the young cowboy not to give her away.

Anyway, he had accompanied her home and found Sam Ford getting a search party ready. The truth of the matter was evident without having to be spelled out by anyone, and when Ginny had dried her tears Sam Ford thanked the youngster and invited him to call at the house any time he happened to be passing.

From that moment the friendship between the young cowboy and the rancher's daughter had ripened, and later it was Johnny Carver who escorted Ginny Ford to the dances in town, to the Fourth of July celebrations, and who was her companion of an evening on leisurely riding trips into the far-flung corners of the range.

He supposed they would marry and settle down one day. It was Ginny's notion that Johnny would eventually be persuaded to give up working for the law and come to work for her father. Hack Doan, the Bar F foreman, was getting on in years and would soon be compelled to quit. When he did, Ginny would see to it that Johnny stepped into his boots.

That was all fine and rosy as far as it went, Johnny had told himself. But Ginny had not reckoned on the streak of independence in Johnny Carver. He had dreams of his own and ambitions of his own. If he ever went back to punching cows he would like to be in a position to buy in on a partnership, at least. If possible, he would prefer to start a small herd of his own, and in this respect the old Benson layout in Mulehead Valley would have proved worthy of consideration.

Johnny saw nothing to alarm him on the trail to the valley. But a mile short of the rock-barrier entrance he swung sharply to the south, then veered to the north-east. He had no intention of approaching the ranch site as he had done yesterday. The valley was little better than five miles wide, but ran to almost ten miles in length. Part of it was wooded and a good deal of the area that would be required for grazing a sizeable herd was covered with scrub and brush. The first task to be addressed by any genuine cowman would consist of clearing the brush and a fair amount of the scrub timber. Mulehead's chief asset was the creek that tumbled from the high walls to the north and meandered for some three miles along the valley floor before twisting towards the wooded country to the south.

A man with vision would alter the course of the creek and possibly amplify that improvement by digging several irrigation ditches. As a consequence there would be more grass of a quality good enough for fodder.

Johnny entered the valley through one of the numerous notches that slashed the rocks like the teeth of a saw. At this point he judged he was a little more than a hundred yards to the west of the main building. Emerging to the open and exercising the utmost care, he saw that he had gauged the situation reasonably well. He had a clear view of one corner of the ranch-house itself, the weeded back yard, the barn and horse corral.

The first thing to attract his attention was a thin spiral of smoke drifting from the chimney pipe, then he switched his gaze to the horses in the corral. He counted six head of stock and a quick thrill ran through him. Here was conclusive evidence that all the strangers belonged to the one band. For reasons of their own they had chosen to drift into Stockwell separately; at least the first three had done so. Perhaps the four who had come to town latterly were bolder than the others, or it might be the way they had it planned.

So far, Johnny had seen no sign of anyone, but the fire in the kitchen stove would testify to their cooking food for breakfast. Supposing he could worm his way closer to the ranch-house? It had not been his original intention; he had started off with the idea of simply ascertaining that the whole gang was congregated here.

Well, they were here, without doubt, so he should back-track at once and head for town. He could report to Hab Beely, when he and the sheriff would plan their next move. Hab would frown at his going any further on his own initiative. Still, it would be to everyone's advantage if he had a clear-cut indication of what the strangers were planning.

Johnny quelled an attack of nervousness and studied the terrain between the spot where he crouched and the gable of the ranch-house. There were plenty of boulders, patches of catclaw. Three big cottonwoods dominated the section directly to the west of the main building. He brought the bay well in to the notch in the rocks and tied the reins to a stunted juniper. He patted the beast's head before leaving it.

'Wish me luck, boy.'

He went up the slope swiftly enough, ducking from boulder to brush clump, from brush clump to boulder. Soon he was close to where the cottonwoods threw gloomy shade from the struggling sunlight. He grabbed a breath and made the final dash. As he came in at the gnarled trunk of a spreading tree he heard the door of the house creak open. He froze then, berating himself for a fool. They must have already eaten breakfast and be in the process of setting out somewhere. His right hand clawed for the gun at his hip as a voice sang out.

'Looks a right fine morning, fellas. I'll go see how the nags are faring.'

Next, Johnny heard boots clump across the porch, the bleached boards creaking in protest. He saw a man stride to the corner of the building, battered stetson thrust to the crown of his head, a cigarette drooping from his lips. One of the four strangers who had ridden into Stockwell. The man contin-ued to the rear of the house and went from view.

Johnny cuffed his brow. He considered the risk of withdrawing immediately and hurrying back to his gelding in the rocks. But something told him to wait, to be careful. The man might return to the house when he had seen to the horses. He was whistling shrilly. The horses in the corral whickered and stamped, and the man laughed.

Johnny stood where he was, waiting. He dare not look out in case he was spotted. Suddenly the man at the corral shouted.

'Hey, Mike!'

'What's eating you, Clem?'

'Come on over here a minute.'

Followed much grunting and the scraping of boots. The sallow-skinned, moustached stranger rounded the corner of the house. He peered this way and that before heading for the corral and going beyond Johnny's range of vision. Johnny heard a low-pitched exchange, then the two fell silent and he felt a prickling at the nape of his neck. He was sure they had noticed something and suspected an intruder was loose in the valley.

Footsteps sounded again and he knew the two were shifting away from the corral, angling out from the corner of the main building. Johnny tried to still the mad thumping of his heart. He eased his Colt from leather. If he acted at once he might get the drop on them. But there was the rest of the outfit in the house to consider, and if it came to a shoot-out he would be the loser when the smoke had cleared.

Instinct told him that he must retreat, gain that boulder behind him. And from there he could hammer off to where he had left his bay.

'*Run like blazes, you fool!*'

He ducked and dashed away from the spreading cover of the cottonwood. He had gone about six yards when someone screeched a warning.

'Hold it or you're dead!'

Johnny skidded to a halt, fighting an urge to blast at the speaker and risk the consequences. Cold reason prevailed, however, and it was as well that it did. Mike and the man called Clem had their six-guns levelled on him and the wonder was that they did not shoot him down where he stood.

'That's showing sense . . . Now, drop your iron *pronto*.'

A second's hesitation while the deputy fought a battle with his raw impulses; then his revolver was slipping from his fingers. By now the others had spilled from the main building in a bunch — the lanky Lute Bannon, the short, squat figure of Fred Post, and the remaining two who had ridden into town with Clem and Mike.

'It's the tin badge from town!' Lute Bannon exulted. 'Well, just look at that . . . Here we are, acting like peaceable critters, and here comes a lawhound sneaking up on us without a by-your-leave! Guess I'd better settle his hash,' he added in a fierce undertone.

'No,' Mike stayed him. 'I happen to be running this show, buster.'

They described a wide, loose circle that held the unfortunate deputy in its centre. Johnny cuffed his brow, told himself that if he was going to die he might as well do it with some dignity. The squat Fred Post gathered up his revolver and shoved it under his waistband. His lips curled as he looked towards the inlet the deputy had used.

'Reckon the tin star's travelling alone?' And to Johnny while the gun centred on his forehead: 'How many more are out there, mister?'

Johnny forced himself to meet the gelid eyes. 'I'm on my own,' he replied steadily.

'Maybe you are and maybe you ain't. My old paw said never to trust a gent that went around with a piece of tin pinned to his shirt.'

'Easy, Fred,' the sallow-faced Mike chided. He was evidently the leader of the bunch and had a crafty look about him that anyone with an ounce of sense would distrust immediately. He gestured to two of his scowling friends. 'Pete, Seth, saddle nags and head down through the rocks. See where he left his horse and if he brought company.'

The two nodded and cut out for the corral. Johnny rubbed his jaw, motioning with his head. 'My horse is just across there. You won't find anybody else around.'

'What brung you here?' Fred Post demanded. 'Reckon you must have heard how I bought this spread from Mr Glover in town yesterday?'

'I heard,' Johnny agreed drily. He pulled his gaze back to Mike. 'For gents who aim to take up cow-raising, you're all acting powerful funny. Sime Cowley was one of your pards, wasn't he?'

'You take it right, Deputy,' Mike said with an emphatic nod. 'Story goes you drilled Sime at the front of that saloon. A damned liar claimed Sime went for his iron first. What have *you* got to say about that?'

'Your pard wouldn't be dead if he hadn't pulled first,' was Johnny's cool response. He would get nowhere by betraying his uneasiness. Hardcases like these respected cold nerve more than they respected cold reason. 'You want to know what brought me out here this morning?' he added with a rougher note. 'I'll tell you. Curiosity, for a start. Bannon hit town yesterday and made trouble in Darton's saloon. We had to run him in.'

'He told me,' Mike said with a thin smile. 'Then you really built a head of steam and bored Sime. You must have quite a reputation in your bailiwick, lawman. So you got curious about us. You found out that Fred had clinched a deal for Mulehead Valley with that land shark. Maybe you don't believe we intend going into the cow business?'

'I've got my doubts,' Johnny confessed. 'You appear to be the head man of the outfit, Mike. Would you give a straight answer to a straight question?'

A hint of grudging admiration tempered the look Mike bent on him. The hardcase fingered his narrow moustache. 'Let's hear it,' he invited. 'But don't forget this is a free country, mister. Man can do pretty much as he pleases. Ain't that so?'

'Within the bounds of the law,' Johnny countered swiftly.

'Law hell!' Lute Bannon ranted. 'I've had a sample of your law, Tin Badge. Right up to my chin!'

'I done told you, Lute,' Mike rebuked. After a heavy pause he said: 'Go ahead and ask your question, Deputy.'

'Are you going to start ranching here in Mulehead?'

'No concern of yours,' was the curt dismissal. 'We can run cows here if we want to. We can run sheep if we want to. Hell, we can do anything we want.'

Johnny fished for makings and set about building a smoke. He was aware of the dark menace posed by these men. They could shoot him where he stood and hide his body somewhere. He might never be seen again. He gulped over the first mouthful of smoke.

'Maybe you've got a point,' he conceded with a tight smile.

'Damn right I have, mister.'

Pete and Seth came into view, leading

Johnny's bay. Seth declared that the deputy must be telling the truth about riding solo.

Fred Post moved closer. 'Guess we can take care of this problem here and now, Mike? I've a score to settle with this one.'

Mike's eyes glittered like beads in his pale, unhealthy face. 'Give the lawdog back his gun,' he commanded.

'What! Are you *loco*, Mike. If we don't — '

'Give him his gun, I tell you. And keep your yap shut.'

Fred Post was obliged to hand the revolver over and Johnny slid the weapon into its holster. He suspected that Mike was figuring out the best tack to suit his own ends.

'What now?' he said to the pale-skinned man.

'Get on your horse and drift. I guess you came out here to talk, but we haven't time to dicker right now. Maybe we'll invite you back later for a pow-wow. Until then, mister, stay out of this valley. Understand?'

Johnny breathed a stream of smoke down his nostrils and flipped his cigarette away. He checked the bay's girth before stepping into the saddle. 'You're cutting a pretty wide swathe, Mike. The way I see it, you'll get along better if you cooperate with the law.'

'I'll certainly think about that. But look at it from my side of the fence, Deputy. The law locked one of my boys in a cell, fined him money he needed to buy grub.' His tone hardened. 'And don't forget either that the law killed another of my pards. Story goes it was a fair do, but I'm not so sure it was.'

'You can take it from me it was a fair do.'

'I need to know for sure, mister. Now, me and my associates have got business to talk over, so hit the trail. And like I said, don't come back till you get an invite. That fat party with the sheriff's badge ain't welcome either. Get the drift, friend?'

'I think I understand your drift, Mike.'

Johnny kneed his bay forward, angling for the main outlet that would give him the easiest access to the town trail.

9

Johnny listened to the bleep and blast of the midnight freight train as it pulled out for the south-west.

The echoes of the whistle in the darkness had a lonesome melancholy appeal. People used trains to make long journeys, to get away from something or some place; or maybe they wanted to find somebody or some new place. Either way, they were driven by a feverish urge, hounded by a disaffection, or drawn by some allure of the unknown.

Seldom did Johnny indulge in philosophising, but tonight he reflected on the years behind him and speculated on what the future might hold if he continued as deputy sheriff in this county.

The truth was that humiliation rankled in him like a poison, had done so ever since he rode away from Mulehead Valley that morning. There was no point in saying one thing and thinking another: the hardcase Mike Wheeler and his friends had sent him back to town with his tail between his legs. And he had been lucky to return in one piece.

He had not travelled far from the valley when he sensed he was being followed at a distance. Often he had drawn the bay gelding to a halt and squinted through the brassy morning sunlight. The land had purported to be empty and innocent, but the sensation had persisted, and only when he arrived at the outskirts of Stockwell did he find release from the almost intolerable strain.

He had expected Hab Beely to be angry, and he was. But there was no use withholding what had happened from the sheriff. His was the main responsibility for law and order, and in the final reckoning Hab would be obliged to answer to the town fathers and the scattered ranchers who had cast their votes for him.

Yet, when the sheriff had simmered down, Johnny could see that he was pleased in a way that he had acted as he did. At least, they now knew that all those strangers shared some common aim. They had come to this neck of the woods for a specific purpose, and any reasonably intelligent observer could deduce that they were not planning a Sunday School picnic.

'What the hell *do* they want with the Benson ranch?' Hab had demanded in a fit of frustration.

'I don't know, old-timer. But I've got a right good suggestion to make. Wire the law officers at the seats of the surrounding counties. Put through descriptions of all seven — even the dead Cowley, too. Mention the names that we know them by, then wait and see what happens.'

Hab had gone off promptly to do this. He had been angrier still at not having thought of it himself. He had given Johnny a meagre grin.

'I'm glad you're packing the badge, boy. Shows the taste I've got. And listen, Mr Carver, sir, you forget about Ginny Ford and her paw's ranch until we see the heels of these *hombres*.'

'Don't worry, Boss. I won't run out on you. Anyhow, I've just about made up my mind to buy the Mulehead Valley place when Post and his sidekicks are through with it.'

All this was flitting through his brain as he strolled to the eastern outskirts of town where the railroad lines described arteries of dull silver in the first faint starlight. He was convinced that the pale-faced Mike and his bunch of hardcases had no intention of going into cattle ranching. They wanted a place to serve as headquarters that was far enough from town to discourage the curious. They were planning some devilry — it didn't need a lot of intelligence to work that out; the problem lay in discovering the nature of that devilry.

It had occurred to Johnny earlier that this could be a rustler outfit, and that in a short time there would be a spate of cattle-thieving on the range. Again, he had viewed the men as being on the run from the law in another territory. It had been a sound idea to have the sheriff make a check in the neighbouring counties, but even then there was no guarantee that they were known and marked.

Johnny chatted with the station agent for a while as he often did when he was too restless to turn in early. He also made it a practice to be at the station when cattle were being loaded for transport to the eastern markets. He left the agent at length and strolled on through the mauve shadows that had begun to mantle the loading pens. He climbed on to a fence rail and was reaching for his tobacco sack when a scuffle in the darkness behind him caused him to freeze.

Something else registered also. He had noticed a couple of men strolling behind him on Main Street a short time earlier. He had been too preoccupied to pay much attention to them, and of course he had no reason to suspect anything out of the ordinary.

Suspicion stirred in him now, breeding the first pricklings of anxiety. He pushed the tobacco sack back into his pocket and turned to probe the gloom shrouding the area.

'Who's there?' His voice sounded oddly weak and hollow in the silence. The air carried a hint of cattle and locomotive oil. Soot from the stack of the departed train had begun to waft and settle. But these were smells well known to him and in no ways objectionable.

His challenge elicited no answer and he shrugged, thinking it might have been a scavenging mutt or a rat. He came off the post slowly, trying to rid himself of the sensation of being under surveillance. Then it came again — a scuffling reminiscent of dragging feet. The noise was out on his left now and he was certain that no dog or rat was responsible.

'Who's there? You'd better speak up — ' The words tailed off as he swung to face the pens straggling drunkenly on his right. Panic hit him but he controlled it. He saw two dim figures. They had split and were on either side of him. What did they want? Why were they following him? Why did they not answer his call?

He stood, rooted so as not to make any noise, listening for a further scuffle that might indicate a definite direction. Across yonder in the darkness he could see the faint glimmer of the lamp in the station agent's quarters. Adam Burley would soon be closing up and going home. There would be no more trains until morning. Even as the thought touched him the lamp in Burley's office was extinguished, and a moment later he heard a door slamming.

He could hail Burley, a man in his late fifties, strong and able, who would be more than willing to come to his aid.

Johnny gritted his teeth, shook his head involuntarily. He had learnt long ago to stand on his own legs. Besides, Burley was married with a couple of children. His wife would be waiting for him, keeping his supper warm on the stove.

Johnny listened to the dim scrape of the station agent's feet as he walked towards the town's outskirts. A horse whickered somewhere back yonder, outside a saloon. There came a low, brisk thunder of hooves as some cowhand loped off to take the trail home. Then nothing.

The silence lasted for what seemed an age. Johnny had not flinched from the spot by the fence rails. The shipping pens described a tangle of these slats, with runways in between. He wiped sweat from his brow, brought his gun to hand, and moved over to the left. He chose a trampled track and went along it. There was a veritable network of these paths and ample space for holding a thousand head of cattle.

Something moved in front of him and he halted. He screwed up his eyes and fancied he saw a shifting shadow, but he could not be sure. The movement behind him took him completely off guard. He spun, panic feeding the raw fury that engulfed him. There was a flurry of running feet behind him and he whirled yet again. The pair of them launched themselves simultaneously. He heard a hard expulsion of breath. Balled fists snaked out, pounding and pummelling. They raked his face, his ribs, his stomach.

Johnny was driven to his knees before that first savage onslaught. He reeled off balance and a boot crashed into his ribs. He scrabbled for his revolver, succeeded in hauling it out, only to have it sent flying from his fingers.

A kick from behind threw him into the filth on his hands and knees. A fist clubbed the side of his head. Two more wicked kicks were delivered. The night became a torment of seething shadow, whistling breath, and the mighty grunting of his attackers.

'Last warning, fella. Keep your nose clean.' To his companion: 'Run like hell.'

Then they were flailing off along the runway and were soon lost in the devouring darkness. Johnny lay for a while before trying to pull himself together. He reached a crouching position but spilled down again, retching and miserable. His ribs ached with every breath and the walls of his skull throbbed. He clawed around in the dirt for his .45, failed to find it. The booted feet dissolved into the agony that consumed him.

He was trying to sit up when he heard other running feet, coming towards the loading pens. He had heaved himself erect and was propped against a warped upright by the time the runner thumped up. Eyes glistened curiously.

'What's wrong? Who is it?'

Johnny recognised Adam Burley's voice. He could have hugged the station agent. He essayed a ragged laugh. 'It's me, Adam. The biggest sucker in the whole territory.'

Burley caught him as he slid sideways, held him until he steadied. 'Johnny! What happened? I locked up and was off for home. Then I remembered letters I wanted to take to the post office in the morning. I heard a racket — '

'Did you see them?'

'I heard somebody running for the sheds over yonder. No, I didn't see them. Who were they?'

'I don't know . . . Thanks, Adam. I'm all right now. No real damage done.'

'I'm not so sure.' Burley held on to his shoulder. 'Look,' he said decisively, 'I'm going to see you to your hotel. Argue if you like, but it won't matter. Want me to take word to Hab?'

'No, no,' Johnny protested. 'I'll see Hab myself in the morning. My gun, Adam . . . Can you find it?'

Burley soon recovered the weapon. Johnny insisted he could make the hotel under his own steam, but the older man was adamant.

'What about your letters then?' Johnny reasoned, hoping to get rid of him.

'I'll collect them later.'

By the time they reached the main drag Johnny was much steadier on his feet. He was pretty sure he had suffered nothing worse than a sound drubbing. No bones were broken, no lasting damage done. Which was just too bad for the hardcases who had dished out the punishment.

Adam Burley not only escorted him into the hotel lobby but took him up the stairs to his room and got the lamp burning. He suggested bringing Doc Cooper, just in case.

Johnny shook his head emphatically. 'I'll be right as rain come morning. I'm fine, I tell you.'

'In a pig's ear,' Burley scoffed. 'But you wouldn't be packing that badge if you didn't know your own mind.'

Johnny was left alone at last. He

stripped off and washed gingerly. There was an ominous dark patch in the region of his left ribs; his stomach muscles ached. He dried off and considered calling down to the night man for a drink. Instead, he let himself sag on to the bed. He was soon asleep and host to a dozen nightmares.

★　★　★

He awoke at dawn to a peremptory rapping on the door. He blinked and spoke thickly.

'It's not locked.'

He expected to see the desk clerk, anxious to know how he was before going off duty, but the visitor was a wrathful Hab Beely.

'You blasted fool,' was the sheriff's terse preamble as he closed the door with his heel and crossed the room to peer out of the window. 'What's the jig?' he added, turning to glare at his deputy. 'You want to keep everything to yourself — is that it? Did somebody tell you I'm not capable of doing my job any more?'

Johnny flung his blanket aside. He was pleased to discover he was in better condition than he had expected to be. 'What little bird told you?'

'Adam Burley dropped by on his way to the station. Figured he ought to rap me up and tell me what happened. Why in hell didn't he tell me last night?'

Johnny forced a deprecatory grin. 'My fault, Hab. I told him not to bother you. What did Burley say?'

It was obvious that the sheriff had dressed hurriedly and had not bothered to fasten all his shirt buttons. He needed a shave.

'Not a whole lot,' he grunted. 'You ran into bother in the station yard. Is that it?'

Johnny explained while he washed and dressed. He had taken a walk to the shipping pens, simply to look around and smoke a cigarette. Hab Beely's face darkened.

'What's so special about raking

through that smell?' he asked suspiciously. 'You really going crazy in the head, like I figure?'

Johnny continued his story. The pair who had dogged him had tricked him and thrown him off guard. 'Then they tackled me with their fists and boots . . . '

Concern replaced the stout lawman's annoyance. 'Well, you don't look all that bad. But how do you feel?'

'Just a mite sore and stiff.' He examined his face in the looking glass and decided he could skip shaving. Beely edged towards the door.

'Why did they tackle you? Must have been some reason?'

'That gang, Hab. They'd like to scare me white so I'll stand back and let them do what they like.'

The sheriff considered him for a moment. Then: 'You having breakfast downstairs or over in Ma's?'

'Guess I'll eat downstairs. Join me if you haven't eaten yet.'

During their meal Johnny enlarged

on what he had found out and what he judged to be on the cards. 'They're planning something really big. That much I'm sure of. They want me to lie low until they make their play.'

'What do they call thumping you around?' Beely retorted sourly. 'You know what this means, son? They'll kill you if you don't back off.'

'They can sure as hell try,' Johnny rejoined grimly. 'But I've hit them once and I can hit them again. And this proves that I know how to hurt them.'

★　★　★

They waited for two days, expecting some of the strangers to show up in town. Johnny went to see Ray Glover and inquire whether Fred Post had met the amount standing on the Mulehead Valley deal. To his surprise and disappointment, he learned that Post had called on the morning after the station yard attack. He had paid the balance in cash and was now the legal owner of the Benson ranch layout.

'You've nothing to be afraid of from those gents, Johnny,' Glover said confidently. 'They claim they're going to raise prime beef stock, maybe a few horses. But, naturally, if the time comes when Post wants to sell . . . '

Johnny was in no mood for pleasantries. 'So Post really said they're going to raise cattle?'

'Yes, he did. But he also said they had no intention of hurrying things just to impress anyone. Their idea is to start out on the right foot with the right stuff.'

If the land agent was impressed, his listener certainly was not. Despite the warnings and the sneak attack under cover of darkness, Johnny ventured out to Mulehead Valey the following day. He found a vantage point in the higher cliffs where he could watch the ranch with the aid of binoculars. All seven horses were in the corral at the rear, for by then Sime Cowley's horse had been recovered from the livery in town. Sime had been buried without ceremony in the local cemetery.

Johnny maintained his vigil until darkness. He saw the men leave the ramshackle ranch-house and ride off down the valley. They returned in an hour, turned their horses loose, and went inside again.

The first glimmering starlight was silvering the sky before the deputy returned to the spot where he had picketed his bay. He mounted and took a roundabout route to reach Stockwell.

10

During the next few days replies to Hab Beely's wire filtered through to the telegraph office. None of the names mentioned by the sheriff was on the 'Wanted' lists of any of the neighbouring counties. But physical descriptions were never much to go on; an outlaw reported with a scar or a beard two months ago might be described as clean-shaven and clear-skinned today. Also, there was always the chance that the newcomers had drifted in from much further afield.

Johnny was not really surprised at the results, although he had hoped that something solid might be forthcoming on at least one of the strangers. Of the bunch out at Mulehead Valley he labelled the man Mike as the most ruthless and therefore the most dangerous. Mike had something up his sleeve and it simply had to be something big. Why else would the seven of them have chosen to rendezvous in Stockwell? And why had they picked on Saul Darton's saloon, except someone had mentioned it as a rendezvous?

Never one to put a black mark against a man's name without reasonable justification, Johnny, nevertheless, had an interview with Saul Darton himself. Darton was sixty, red-faced and portly, he drank a fair amount of the better class of liquor that he bought for his saloon. He was also a trifle short-tempered, and it didn't take long for him to divine the reason for the deputy's visit.

'Now, you lookit here, Carver,' he said in his exaggerated drawl, 'why don't you stop beating around the bush and get it off your chest? Everybody's talking about the gents holed up in Mulehead. They're wondering why they're there and what they're aiming to do. It's got around as well that they picked my place as a water-hole. And now you come along with your veiled hints . . . '

'No, you're wrong, Saul,' Johnny objected hastily. 'I'm not hinting at anything. I'm just doing my job the best I can. Any lawman would ask himself why they breezed in on your place. All I'm saying is, have you any ideas that might be helpful?'

'No, I haven't,' Darton said flatly. 'You should have come right out with it in the first place instead of straining yourself to leave a false trail. Now, you tell me something, boy, before we go any further: do I look like a man would be in cahoots with a bunch of crooks?'

'Of course not.' Johnny had bother curbing his anger. His cheeks had gone almost as ruddy as Darton's. 'I'm just trying — '

'Yes, sir, I know, I know! I'm not taking offence. I've always admired you, as a matter of fact. You did right to plant a slug in that Cowley bird. It has put you up a notch in my esteem. But please, Johnny Carver,' he added with a tortured smile, 'don't figure I'm a friend of these sidewinders.'

'Saul, you know I didn't — '

Darton laughed boisterously and waved the whole business aside. He offered Johnny a thick Cuban stick and a drink. Johnny felt obliged to accept both as a means of mollifying him. 'As I see it,' Darton enlarged with a broad wink, 'it's simple enough. One of these fellas must have been in town before and remembered my saloon. Or they just heard of Saul Darton's saloon, and that was that.' He patted Johnny's shoulder. 'A man's fame has a way of spreading.'

Johnny nodded and rose to leave. There was a sheen of moisture on his brow. 'I reckon that's it, as you say, Saul. Thanks for the help.'

'Pleasure. Drop in any time you're passing. But, Johnny,' he said quickly as the deputy turned away, 'if I was your age I'd walk across the road and break Ray Glover's neck with my bare hands. He shouldn't have sold them that roost in the first place.'

Later that day, Johnny tried to sneak out of town on another trip to the environs of Mulehead Valley. But Hab Beely was waiting for the move and insisted on going along. They found a relatively safe place in the rocks where they could spy on the ranch with binoculars. This time there were only four horses in the corral, suggesting that three of the strangers had ridden off somewhere.

'Not a damn cow in sight,' Beely muttered, wiping the back of his neck with a handkerchief. 'How do they plan to live if they don't buckle down to work?'

Johnny merely shook his head morosely. He was wondering where the missing owlhooters might be, for by then he knew that they favoured a night-time trade. They had not been in town when he and Hab left, and they had not met anyone on the trail. Then a thought occurred to Johnny that brought an accompanying chill.

Supposing that, while they were keeping this layout under observation, the strangers were hidden up somewhere, keeping an eye on them?

Johnny kept his worry to himself, but now and then, in the course of the next two hours, one or another of the strangers would come out to fetch water from the pump in the yard — Tad Benson had never seen fit to pump water straight into the ranch-house kitchen — or one of them would saunter round to the outhouses at the rear.

Hab and Johnny were in the process of pulling out when they heard hoofbeats coming along the valley from the western end, and soon three riders swept past the rocks where the lawmen were located and headed for the huddle of buildings squatting in the sunshine.

'They've been out on the cattle country somewhere,' Beely observed musingly. 'Maybe sizing up a herd.'

'Maybe,' Johnny conceded. But he did not think so. By then it was common knowledge among the ranchers that a queer outfit had taken up abode in Mulehead Valley, and most cattlemen distrusted strangers until they had good reason for accepting them. Johnny had heard that Sam Ford, among others, had posted nighthawks to guard his stock.

'Come on,' the sheriff said presently when the three had turned their horses into the corral and entered the house. 'There's nothing doing here. Seems we'll have to go on playing the waiting game.'

'I guess you're right, Hab. But I've an idea we won't have to wait much longer.'

★　★　★

Next day, Johnny was emerging from Ma Pearson's cafe after lunch when he halted abruptly and watched the sallow-faced Mike and Lute Bannon ride into town. Johnny was tempted to retreat to the cafe until they went past, but Lute

Bannon had already spied him and spoke quickly to Mike. Johnny eased his shoulders against a sidewalk awning support as the two men drew level.

'Howdy, Mr Deputy!' Mike hailed loudly. They brought their horses to a standstill and the pale-featured man clasped his gloved hands over the horn. 'Say,' he added in a friendly manner, 'maybe you could tell us where we could get a supply of chuck?'

Johnny eyed them steadily for a moment, noting the wariness in the lanky, stoop-shouldered Bannon. He held the reins in his left hand while the fingers of his right hand rested on his hip, mere inches from the butt of his holstered revolver.

Johnny answered coldly: 'I'd have thought you were wise to *all* the tricks by now, mister.'

'Call me Mike,' the other invited, not rattled in the least. 'Mike Wheeler's the handle, mister. Seeing as how I might be in this neck of the woods for a considerable spell, we might as well get acquainted. But what's this about tricks?' he added in a puzzled fashion. 'You're saying you didn't get a fair do when you rambled into Mulehead Valley?'

'I'm not talking about Mulehead now. I'm talking about your style the other night at the railroad station.'

What anyone would have read as genuine amusement brightened the sharp eyes for a second. Then Wheeler flung a sidelong glance at Bannon.

'You know what he's talking about, Lute?'

'No, I don't,' the lanky man said, touching his lips with the tip of his tongue. 'You're talking in riddles, Deputy. What happened at the railroad station? Somebody let the steam out of the loco?' He laughed, but it was obvious that Mike Wheeler failed to share his amusement.

'You're sure you're as green as you claim, Lute?' he asked ominously.

'Hell, I am, Mike. Quit riding me, will you? The lawjohn don't like us, and that's that. He's ready to say anything about us. The way he downed Sime — '

'Forget Sime,' Wheeler barked. He lifted his hands from the saddlehorn, shook out his reins. 'You forget it as well, Deputy. We'll ask somebody else about supplies. Thanks for nothing, Carver.'

They drifted on past and Johnny released a slow, tight breath. The pair pulled in opposite the Cowbell saloon. They had racked their mounts and gone into the building when Hab Beely appeared from the store doorway just diagonally across the road from Johnny. The stout sheriff clumped through the road dust.

'Was watching those *hombres* real close,' he observed. 'What was all that air-warming about?'

'They're in town for supplies. It's what they claim anyway. I dropped a hint about what happened at the station yard.'

'Bastards who jumped you ought to be drawn and quartered,' Beely said with a bleak scowl. 'How did they react?'

'Mike let on he didn't know what I was talking about. Could be he doesn't know. But that cross-eyed pard of his knows for sure. It's plain that Wheeler's holding the reins. All the same, Hab, I'm convinced that Bannon was one of them. Post could have been the other, wanting to teach me a lesson. Maybe they decided to tackle me without saying anything to the big chief.'

'The Wheeler bird, you mean?'

'That's what I mean.' Johnny let his smouldering gaze shuttle to the horses outside the Cowbell. 'That white-faced character could have been locked up for a long time, or maybe he's got lung trouble. But he's as sly as a fox and plenty dangerous.'

'Hell, I know that.'

The lawmen stayed where they were until the pair from Mulehead Valley left the saloon ten minutes later. They mounted up and headed for the livery stable, and when they came out Lute

Bannon was on the driving seat of a buckboard, with his horse running on a fairly lengthy rope. Mike Wheeler rode out front and they both finished up opposite the loading bay of Munster's general store.

Johnny and Hab watched them load enough foodstuffs to keep an average cow outfit going for a week. They called at a few other stores, and when their business was finished they set off the way they had come.

Hab Beely heaved a sigh and scratched the back of his neck speculatively. 'Just supposing we've got these fellas figured wrong? How does it all strike you?'

'Same as before,' Johnny drawled. 'And I've got enough bruises to back that opinion.'

Half an hour later the sheriff was obliged to make a further adjustment to his sentiments concerning the strangers. Mart Aldred, who traded in guns, ammunition and the like, visited his office.

'Hab, those two gents who were in town a while ago . . . ' was his diffident preamble.

'The fellas from Mulehead Valley?' Beely urged with an arched brow. 'I saw them in town. They bought shells from you, maybe?'

'They bought shells, sure,' Aldred told him. 'But they were asking for something else, and when I took a while to think it over I thought I'd better tell you about it.'

'Say, that's great,' Beely commended drily. 'What took you so long to make your mind up, Mart?'

'They asked me if I could supply them with a few sticks of dynamite.'

'What!' If Aldred had sought to rock the portly lawman he succeeded. Then, in a hoarse whisper: 'Did they say what they aim to do with the dynamite?'

'They seem to figure the water out at Mulehead isn't running in the right direction,' the storekeeper explained with a scornful laugh. 'I mulled it over after they left and wondered if they were just pulling my leg.'

'So they weren't really serious about the dynamite?'

'Oh, they sounded serious enough.'

Beely looked through the street window and grimaced as if in pain. 'But damn it, Mart, you don't stock dynamite. There's a town ordinance says it can't be stored within a mile of this burg. You don't have any hidden in a cellar, I hope?'

'Course not. When the ranchers want stuff to shift rocks or make a dam I put an order through for the quantity ordered and no more.'

'You didn't say you'd order some for them?'

'Heck, Sheriff, I had to say it could be done. Anyhow, they told me to forget it and they'd ask someplace else.'

Beely thanked the storekeeper and accompanied him to the street. He found Johnny Carver at the smith's place, watching a big farm horse being shod.

'Why, hello, Hab. Want a new set of

heels for your boots?'

'Come on outside, boy.' At the yard pump, Beely related what he had learnt from Mart Aldred. Johnny blew a shrill whistle.

'Dynamite! What do they want that for?'

'You tell me,' the sheriff growled. 'They told Mart they wanted to alter the course of the creek out in Mulehead. Would that figure?'

'Yes, it might,' the deputy answered slowly. 'It's how I see the creek myself. If I moved into the valley I'd want more water flowing east. But my idea would be to dig irrigation ditches.'

'Have these galoots never heard of picks and shovels?'

'Picks and shovels would do the trick, Boss. It would be slower, though, and mean losing some gravy.'

'Quit fooling around, damn it. So you're saying the dynamite ain't for altering the course of the creek?'

'No, it isn't,' Johnny answered firmly. He rubbed his jaw and considered for a minute. 'Just supposing this is all part of their game, and they're trying to keep us running in circles?'

'You mean the dynamite is just so much talk to keep burrs under our saddles? I don't understand that, but then I might be dimmer than I figured.'

'Look, old-timer, they deliberately go to Mart and ask about thunder sticks. They know the sort of talk that's going to start around the town. They know Mart will get worried and tell us about it. So it looks like just another trick to keep us on our toes.'

'That sounds like nonsense to me,' Beely declared with dark suspicion. 'You've got something else under your hat.'

'Hab, you can see what they're up to as well as I can. They're out to keep us sitting on the edge of a knife, scare the hell out of us. And maybe scare the whole town at the same time. But yes, I'd like to know if they're really keen to get their hands on dynamite . . . '

★ ★ ★

Something else was to turn up later in the day. Jim Styles, one of Sam Ford's cowhands, brought in letters to be left at the post office. The rangy Styles took the opportunity to grab a drink in Darton's saloon before heading back home, and on his way out he ran into Johnny Carver.

'Oh, hello, Johnny,' the cowboy greeted, 'was just going to find you. Boss asked me to look you up. He said if you ain't too busy he'd like you to drop past and say hello.'

Johnny didn't bother hiding his surprise. He asked if anything was the matter back home, but the laconic Jim said if there was he hadn't heard of it.

'Sam's well enough?' Johnny pursued.

'Fighting fit, I'd say.' He grinned. 'Say, Johnny, if you've got any influence with Mr Ford, maybe you'd tell him not to drive us critters so hard.'

'I'll remember that. You do look like a

gent being worked to skin and bones. What about Ginny, Jim?'

'Purty as ever. But don't you keep her waiting too long, Mr Lawjohn, else one of us real handsome boys will snatch her clear out of your arms.'

Johnny punched his chest. 'Tell Sam I'll call by in the morning. Seriously, you don't think I ought to visit sooner?'

The tall cowboy sobered, pushed a wing of dark hair under his hat. 'Can't say that for a fact. Boss is a closed-mouthed *hombre* at the best of times. You should know that by now.'

'Course I do.' Johnny reached a decision. 'Give me a minute to speak to Hab and I'll head out with you.'

He told the sheriff what had transpired and that he would be back as quickly as he could make it. 'Sam wouldn't send that sort of message if there wasn't more to it. Maybe cows missing or something suchlike.'

Hab Beely's eyes glinted. 'If that's what's troubling Sam Ford then we'll have a better idea what that bunch in Mulehead Valley's up to.'

★   ★   ★

In a little more than an hour later Johnny and Jim Styles arrived in the front yard of the great sprawling ranch layout that was Sam Ford's chief pride after his daughter. It was Ginny who emerged to greet Johnny, and if the girl knew anything about her father's message her reaction gave no indication of the fact.

'What brings you out here?' she asked with genuine surprise. 'Nothing wrong in town, I hope?'

'No more than usual. I guess you heard how I had to match guns with a *hombre*?' he asked gravely. It was something he wished to dispose of quickly.

'Yes, I heard.' Her fingers touched his arm and remained there for a moment. Her eyes raced over his face. 'You've been hurt. Those strange men in

Mulehead Valley . . . Johnny, why don't you quit that job and start riding for dad?'

Johnny essayed a weak laugh. He was glad to see Sam Ford clatter down the porch steps with Hack Doan, his foreman. Ford strode over, right hand extended.

'Pleased to see you, young fella. Called to pass the time of day, I guess?'

Something in the way he said that told Johnny to be careful. He nodded, shrugging at the same time. 'That's the size of it, Sam. Maybe you've got a glass of root beer to spare?'

'You bet . . . Honey, you can talk to Johnny later, huh? He looks like a plumb thirsty gent to me. Come through to my den, Johnny, and I'll fetch that beer. See you later, Hack.'

Johnny nodded and when he turned to throw a salute to Ginny he found her watching him with an odd look in her eye. He swung and followed the rancher into the house while his foreman went about his business.

11

Sam Ford left Johnny in his office and
came back with an earthenware pitcher,
or *olla*, and two glasses. The moonshine
tasted better than Johnny expected and
he mustered a wry smile.

'Hope you don't make this yourself,
Sam. It's just stuff bought in town, isn't
it?'

'Call it rye, if you like,' the burly
rancher grinned. 'No, a friend sent it,
and I didn't like to be discourteous and
refuse it.'

Johnny lighted the cigar Ford gave
him and blew a stream of rich smoke.
'There's a problem, Sam? You're not
missing cattle?'

'Rustlers?' Ford laughed and shook
his head. 'Nothing like that. I'm sorry if
you got the idea I wanted to see you in
a hurry.'

'All right then,' Johnny said, eyeing

him steadily. 'So there's no hurry. But I just happened to be out this way and remembered what Jim Styles said about a call.'

'That's handsome of you, Johnny.' Ford aimed his cream-coloured stetson at a peg and ran his fingers over his thick hair. 'But I believe you and Sheriff Beely have enough on your platters at the minute, what with these drifters taking up residence in Mulehead Valley, and you having to shoot one of them . . .'

'Sam, what the devil is this?' the deputy demanded. 'I know when something's bothering you, and if you don't want me to try and help then I'm just wasting my time sitting here like this.'

'It's to do with Ginny,' the cowman said quietly.

'Ah!' The blood receded from Johnny's face. His throat tightened while his eyes clung to the rancher's craggy features. 'What's the matter with Ginny? She's well, isn't she? She looked well enough when I saw her in town. And just now — '

'She's well enough,' Ford agreed. 'Relax.' He sat down opposite the young lawman and made a steeple with his thick, capable fingers. 'I didn't want her to know the reason I asked you to call. But she's sharp enough and she might guess. When she first told me I laughed it off. But when it happened again I reckoned there could be more to it than her imagination.'

'What the blue hell are you talking about, Sam? If Ginny's in any trouble I ought to know about it. Now quit acting like the cat got your tongue and tell me what's wrong.'

Even then it seemed the rancher had difficulty in conveying what he wished to say. Johnny was to understand this later. The last thing Sam Ford wanted him to think was that Ginny was simply plagued by an over-active imagination.

'The first time was almost a week ago,' he explained. 'You know how she goes riding on her own? The day she has to leave off riding a horse will be the saddest day of her life. Well, anyhow . . . she was over close to Broken Horn Creek when she saw this jasper on a hill-top. She says he just sat there about a quarter-mile off and watched her. She took him to be one of the boys and set out to meet him. But as soon as she did the gent did a disappearing act *pronto*.'

Johnny swallowed hard. He could see what Sam Ford meant. The girl had told her father of the incident when she returned home, but he had merely chuckled at the idea.

'Ginny had no way of knowing who he was?'

'She knows he was a rank stranger. Of course, she couldn't see him clearly at that distance. At the time I told her to forget it and give Broken Horn Creek a pass for a while. Then — the very next day — she was five miles or so to the west of here, and there he was again.'

'The devil you say! The same gent, Sam?'

'Ginny figures so. But she couldn't be sure. He kept that distance, sat his nag on a hill and watched her. This time she got kind of scared. She carries a .32 with her when she's riding, for rattlesnakes, you understand.'

Johnny nodded, his face hard and thoughtful. 'But she didn't shoot at the *hombre*?'

'She said she was tempted to do that. This was when I had the notion she might just be imagining a mysterious horseman. She got mad when I said so. Then she said she wouldn't tell me again, no matter what she saw. I got round her and asked her to promise to keep telling me what happened. Next day, when I saw her head off, I sent Jud Walker to trail her. I gave Jud instructions to keep well out of sight and make sure he spotted this gent if he popped up on any hills.'

'Did he?'

'Sure as anything he did. Jud got an eyeful of him. But Ginny — damned if she didn't lose her nerve and let loose a shot. Jud kept his head. He saw the stranger slide back behind the hill. Jud detoured from Ginny and tried to overhaul the gent. But he got away clean. Five times in all this has happened, Johnny.'

'You should have told me earlier, Sam.'

'Maybe I should. But with all due respects, what could you do that my boys couldn't?'

Johnny shrugged, guessing the real reason.

'Ginny didn't want to bring me into it?' he hazarded.

'She claimed you were pretty busy, what with the drifters in Mulehead Valley. But then I added two and two, and — '

'You think the joker doing the spying could be one of these drifters, Sam? Blazes, you could be right! But why this interest in Ginny?'

Ford pulled a little grimace. 'Might be innocent enough. Maybe the yokel took a fancy to my girl. Still, I don't like it.'

'Neither do I,' Johnny said grimly. 'I guess you'd better warn Ginny to quit riding on her own for a spell.'

'I have. You try talking her out of it if you can.'

'I will,' Johnny promised. 'But you don't want her to know why I'm here?'

Ford shrugged in fatalistic fashion. 'She'll guess. But what do you make of these fellas in the Mulehead, Johnny?'

It was an opening for the deputy to tell the cowman what had happened to date, and when he mentioned the bid to buy dynamite from Mart Aldred the rancher swore softly.

'Dynamite! Why in heck do they want dynamite?'

'They told Mart they wanted to change the course of the creek. Does that make sense to you?'

Sam Ford was slow in giving a reply. He supposed it was possible the men might go into ranching eventually, and they might start clearing the brush and scrub timber and providing a better water supply. But if he were in Johnny's boots he would keep a close eye on them.

'The way that gent made trouble for you in Darton's is a mark against them,' he added. 'The way the gunslinger pushed you into a fight says they're anything but honest cowmen. And then the railroad station attack on you . . . well, it just doesn't square up, and you know it better than I do.'

The sun was arching towards the west when Johnny went outside with the rancher. He looked around for Ginny, but saw no sign of her.

'Better not leave without seeing her,' Sam Ford said with a chuckle. 'She must be in the house.'

When they reached the house, however, they found no trace there either. Ford chewed his underlip glumly. 'Hope she hasn't headed off this time of day. You might find her on the trail, though.'

'I might. I'll see her soon anyhow.

Stay alert, Sam.'

'You bet. And watch that outfit in Mulehead Valley.'

Johnny mounted up and rode out of the yard. He had an odd feeling about Ginny just then. He suspected she knew he was at the ranch and was waiting somewhere to get him on his own. It transpired he was right: at the end of the lane where willows and cottonwoods formed a natural windbreak, the girl stepped out in front of his horse.

'I knew you were getting ready to leave,' she told him with a twinkle in her eye. 'Are you in a hurry back to town?'

'I suppose so.' He dismounted and she began fondling the bay's nose. All the while her eyes probed him, displaying that trace of mischief which he found both annoying and intriguing. 'You know why your dad wanted to see me?' he pressed.

'I guessed,' she said, turning from the horse. 'He told you of the man who has been spying on me?'

'He's worried, honey. There might be reason to worry.'

'I know,' she agreed with a little shiver. 'At first I treated it as a joke. Well, some attractive boy might have been admiring me from a distance, as they say in those novels.'

'It's no joke,' he growled. 'You've no right to treat it as a joke.'

'Why, Johnny Carver! I do believe you're jealous . . . '

'Oh, dang it, Ginny,' he protested. 'It — it's just plain common sense. You quit taking these long rides over the country. You've got your dad worried, and you'll have me worried as well.'

'Truly, Johnny?' She was close to him now, so close he could feel the warmth of her breath on his face. She was in one of those mischievous, irresponsible moods he had never been able to fathom and which he found distinctly disturbing. Her progress from girlhood to womanhood had seemed so rapid and devastating, and he had never ceased to thrill to the baffling complexities that had replaced her earlier simplicity.

'Look, honey, I've got to get back to town. Hab will be waiting for me.'

'You and that fat old sheriff!' Her fingers tightened on his arm. Her red lips were within an inch of his face. The timbre of her voice sent wild vibrations through him. Then she laughed. 'I don't mean any offence to Hab Beely, Johnny. I have the greatest respect for him. After all, he recognised your qualities before a lot of other people did.'

'Please, Ginny . . . '

'You called me honey, Johnny. Was it just a slip of the tongue?'

'I'll call you something different if you don't quit taking these lone rides,' he said sternly.

'But I enjoy taking rides on my own. I might be a tearaway at heart, for all you know — or perhaps care.'

It was one of those occasions when the complexity of Ginny Ford filled Johnny with something akin to dismay.

'Why don't you stop acting child-ishly?' he burst out.

'Do you want me to promise, Johnny?' she countered, unabashed.

'Promise what?' he groaned.

'Just kiss me and I'll consider doing everything exactly as you dictate.'

'Damn you, girl,' he cried huskily.

It was a long time before he had the strength, never mind the inclination, to break away from her. When he finally did he lunged to his bay and hauled himself to the saddle. He brought the big gelding around in a prancing circle, his eyes twin flames of flashing fire.

'Don't you go traipsing by yourself,' he thundered. 'Do you hear me, girl?'

'I hear you, Johnny. Please be careful . . . '

He was off before she could finish, pounding on to the open range beyond the trees and soon going from her sight.

★   ★   ★

It was full dark by the time Johnny reached Stockwell, by which time he had managed to regain his composure. But it would have taken infinitely more than the problem of the strangers in Mulehead Valley to dispel the exhilaration that pounded through every fibre of his being.

He took the bay to the livery stable first of all, rubbed it down and watered it, and put the horse into a stall with a bait of hay.

'No grain till tomorrow, old son. Don't want you spending the night jumping at the moon.'

He went to his hotel room and had a wash before heading to Ma Pearson's cafe for supper. As luck would have it, Hab Beely was just finishing his meal at a table close to the serving hatch. The sheriff was pleased to see him and declared that nothing of moment had taken place in his absence.

'What did Sam Ford want with you?' Hab asked curiously then. 'You look like a gent has been offered a partnership in a gold mine. Ford offered you the ramrod's job, I take it?'

'Not so fast,' Johnny chided with a grin. 'Sam isn't as hard up for a crew as you seem to think.' The waiter came and he ordered, and when he had gone he told Hab what Sam Ford had related about the mysterious horseman who was spying on Ginny.

'The devil you say,' the sheriff grunted. 'You're sure Ginny isn't just imagining she's being watched? After all, Sam has a big crew. A lot of young blood — Say, that could be it! One of Sam's leather-slappers has taken a shine to the girl.'

Eventually Johnny persuaded him that the problem was more serious. Jud Walker had sighted the stranger but had been unable to catch him. Hab thought it over for a few minutes, then he smiled crookedly.

'Just one thing you can do to bring an end to it, mister. Get a rope on the gal and bring her to the preacher. Best

207

way I know to keep a woman out of trouble.'

Johnny's meal came and he commenced eating. Hab pushed his chair back and rose, consulting his watch. 'You had an appointment with Sam Ford. I've got one with Mark Ferris at my office in five minutes. He said he wanted a private word with me when I'd the time to spare.'

'The banker? What's eating Ferris, Hab?'

'Don't know till I see him.' Beely sighed. 'But I've lived long enough to know one thing, boy: trouble never arrives in one parcel. Anyway, don't come near the office till he leaves. He's a bit of a queer bird. Remember the time he figured somebody was trying to dig a tunnel under the bank? This might be another of his crazy notions.'

It suited Johnny to have a leisurely meal. He gave scant thought to Hab's appointment with the banker. Ferris was the only man in town who didn't treat the deputy as an equal. Ferris distrusted youth in whatever form it presented itself. He was well into his sixties and the two tellers he employed were in their fifties. It all added up to his errand boy having a hard time. There was a rumour, too, that the bank wasn't doing too well at the minute.

Johnny put the banker and his staff out of his mind and gave himself to dreaming about Ginny Ford and the future they might have together.

'Like anything else, Johnny?'

He looked up with a start to see the waiter watching him with a tired smile at his lips. 'No, thanks, Jack. Guess you want to get home.'

'Good night, Johnny,' the elderly Ma Pearson called through the serving hatch as he left.

On the street, he stood in the shadows for a while, building a cigarette and watching the comings and goings of the occasional horseman. An hour had passed since Hab left him and he wondered what Mark Ferris could have wanted with the sheriff.

Buck Arden was alone in the law office when he got there. Arden had the checkers laid out on the board and was concentrating deeply.

'Hello, Buck,' Johnny grinned. 'Planning a new way to cheat yourself? Is Hab here?'

'In back.' The elderly man gestured to the door leading through to the sheriff's living quarters. 'He's expecting you.'

Johnny rapped with his knuckles and Hab Beely called for him to enter. He found the sheriff ensconced in an easy chair, pipe on a tray at his elbow. He appeared to be in troubled thought.

'Sit down, Johnny. Fix yourself a cup of coffee. Ferris left a while ago. I told you troubles never came singly, didn't I?'

'What's wrong, old-timer?' Johnny dragged a chair over and sat down. 'One of the tellers been pilfering the bank funds?'

'It isn't funny,' Beely admonished with a scowl. 'This is the twentieth of

210

the month,' he went on, as if relating something from memory. 'In two days' time there'll be a consignment of money — folding stuff and silver and gold coins — coming from Chicago.'

Johnny whistled. 'So that's what the fuss is all about? Ferris is anxious to see it lodged safely in his vaults?'

'One hundred thousand dollars,' Beely continued as if he had not been interrupted. 'But it isn't all for Mark's bank. Some of it has to be re-routed south on the train pulling out on the morning of the twenty-third. There's no through train, as you know, so it means the money's got to be kept in the bank vault overnight.'

'One hundred thousand! Never knew there was that much *dinero* in the country. So we'll be responsible for the consignment for twelve hours or so. Where is it going south — to Gimbal?'

'To Flintburg,' Beely told him. 'It'll have a train guard to here, and another from here to Flintburg. But in between we'll be expected to ride shotgun, and that's what worries me.'

'We'll manage all right, Hab,' Johnny said confidently. 'Once the shipment's in the bank vault it'll be safe enough.'

'Will it?' the sheriff snorted. 'For your information, son, that vault at Ferris' place ain't much stronger than a corned beef can. We've got to keep quiet about this because, if it gets out there's so much money around Stockwell, every crook in the country might start planning how to grab it.'

12

Long after he had gone to bed in his hotel room Johnny lay and thought over what the sheriff had told him. The sum of one hundred thousand dollars in gold, silver, and paper money would be delivered in town on the twenty-second of the month. It would be kept in the bank vault overnight and loaded on to the south-bound spur line the following morning — not too long for a band of ambitious outlaws to formulate a plan, but long enough for a certain calibre of owlhooter.

Johnny smoked cigarette after cigarette — something he never really did. His mind, although restless, seemed to require extra stimulus to keep up with the fleeting thoughts.

A band of six hardcases out in Mulehead Valley. A man following Ginny Ford when she went on her beloved solitary rides. A hundred thousand dollars being lodged in the bank vault in two days' time . . . Where did the pieces fit together? Did they come together, or was he stretching his imagination to a ridiculous limit?

'I guess I'm crazy,' he muttered at length. 'I used to be a level-headed gent, with my boots firmly on the ground. Now I'm figuring like a nervous old lady. Ginny will be all right. Those fellows in Mulehead Valley really do intend going into ranching. As for the money coming into the bank on its way south — it's as good as in the bank at Flintburg.'

He slept at last. He fancied he was in the throes of a nightmare when he awoke suddenly. He could have been sleeping for minutes or for hours. An unusual sound had jarred him awake. Then he realised that the window shade was slightly open and there was a vague, foreign, shape in the shadows.

He was lunging for his Colt when a voice rapped out: 'Don't move, or you're dead! I mean it, Mr Deputy.'

'What — ' Johnny choked. 'Who are you?' His hand had scant inches to travel to reach the revolver in its pouch at the head of the bed, but he refrained from making the short, fast snatch.

'Never mind who I am,' the other advised. 'I know who you are, and that's what matters.'

The voice had a familiar quality, even though the intruder was trying to disguise it. Johnny was sure he could place it, given the time to reflect.

'You come here to kill me?' he said with a hard laugh, playing for a space in which to collect his thoughts. 'I've tramped on your toes, maybe? But if you figure you've — '

'Shut up,' the man rapped. 'Don't try pulling any tricks, Deputy. Don't think I can't see you clear enough, because I can see in the dark as good as in daylight. I don't aim to kill you, 'cept I have to. Killing you'd be an easy chore, I guess. But worse could happen if you don't do what I say.'

'You're talking double Dutch, damn it,' Johnny growled, anger starting to fan through him. 'What could be worse than getting yourself killed?'

'You'll see,' was the cryptic answer. He lowered his tone. 'Are you ready to listen to me, Carver? Because I don't intend spending the rest of the night talking. If you don't do what you're told you're done. Now listen real good: mighty soon you're going to get news that'll upset you, kind of. But that don't mean you've to go hog-wild. You'll keep your head. You'll *remember* what I told you. If you keep cool and don't do anything stupid everything will pan out. Otherwise you're going to be a mighty sorry boy. Understand all that?'

'Like blazes I do!' Johnny erupted. 'Why can't you lay your cards on the table so I can get your drift.'

'You'll see my cards *pronto*, Carver. Then you'd better remember everything I said. Don't try to make a hero of yourself. It won't work. Apart from which, you'll end up dead anyway.'

Johnny saw an arm being drawn back. He recoiled instinctively, rolled across the bed to hit the floor on the other side. He expected to hear a knife blade thrum into the bedding or thunk into the wall. He heard a heavy slap as something did strike the wall, then a quick flurry at the window. The man had gone through to the gallery. Boots scraped briefly. The gallery rail creaked; something landed heavily on the street.

It had all taken place in a matter of seconds. Johnny bounded to his feet, realising he had been fooled. He picked up a lump of rock from the floor. A horse whickered, somewhere close to the hotel. Then hooves were hammering down the road, intent on gaining the end of the main drag.

Johnny grabbed his gun and went to the window. The lower half was open and he stepped through to the gallery. The night intruder was heading for open country at a rapid lick. It would be useless getting dressed, going to the stable for his bay, and trying to follow him.

He stood on the platform for several minutes, the cool breeze blowing through his hair, listening until the night swallowed the diminishing hoofbeats. A mutt barked. Across the way a lamp sprang to life in the living quarters above a store. Before the owner could open the window to investigate Johnny had returned to his room, lowered the window frame, and put the shade in place.

The hotel remained quiet and he was glad of that. The last thing he wanted was any sort of fuss. He needed time to unravel the enigmatic warning, but time itself was running out.

'Mighty soon you're going to get news that'll upset you . . . '

'What did he mean? Who was he — Post, by heaven!' Yes, it just had to be Fred Post. He had done his best to disguise his voice, but there was no doubt that the visitor had been the thick-set stranger. So they really were planning some devil work in Mulehead

Valley. 'And I'm willing to bet it's tied in with the money coming to the bank. But how could that bunch have known about the shipment?'

The question nagged at Johnny. He lifted his watch from the side of the bed and peered at the dial. Just gone three o'clock. Hab Beely would be asleep in his quarters at the back of the law office. Should he stir Hab out and tell him what had happened?

It seemed the sensible thing to do. The sheriff would be angry if he held out on him. And yet, what profit would be gained from worrying Hab at this time of night? Perhaps he should wait a while before making any move, until daylight at least. Fred Post's cryptic warning might amount to nothing more than an arrogant blast of wind. They meant to harass him, unnerve him. He had shot their friend, Sime Cowley, dead and they wanted to square for Cowley in their own way.

But what might he hear to cause him distress?

A vision of Ginny rose to his mind, hovered there; now faint, now terribly clear, her eyes strangely accusing. But it was silly to think of Ginny Ford in the context of the bunch at Mulehead Valley. Yet someone had been following Ginny wherever she went, spying on her. For what reason?

Ten minutes later he was fully dressed. A lot of things could wait, possibly, until daylight came and lent him a clearer perspective. But there was no getting around the fact that he and the sheriff would be solely responsible for the safety of the shipment that would soon reach town, therefore he felt obliged to act as he saw fit.

He settled his hat, buckled his gunbelt on, and headed for the staircase. He was relieved to find the night clerk sleeping soundly at the back of his desk. The clerk had made himself as comfortable as possible and had his feet propped. The street door was closed but not locked. Johnny slipped out and drew the door to behind him.

There was a cold bite to the air at this hour, but it tended to brush the last traces of drowsiness from his brain. He turned east, continuing steadily until he reached the intersection where Lincoln Avenue ran south. He halted at a picket fence half-way along the avenue and surveyed the front of the large house he had arrived at. He hesitated momentarily while doubts crowded in. Then, his jawline firming, he opened the gate and trod the gravel path to the front door.

The house was in darkness, as was the rest of the avenue. There were a few trees here, cottonwoods and live-oaks, and he listened to the faint rustling of foliage in the breeze. He rapped sharply with his knuckles and waited.

A minute went past, another. He rapped again. A candle or lamp flared to life in the hallway. A voice came, querulous and slightly rasping.

'Who's there?'

'Deputy Carver. Open up, Mr Ferris. Sorry to disturb you like this, but I want to talk to you.'

He heard what could have been a low curse, a grumble. A bolt slid back and he was confronted by the bank manager, tousled-haired, clad in a long night-robe and with slippers on his feet. He looked something less than dignified in this early-morning role. There was a glint at the back of his eye, too, that might easily be interpreted as fear.

'Johnny Carver?' he grunted, blinking. 'What on earth's the matter with you? Say, there hasn't been a break-in at the bank?'

'Not yet,' Johnny replied tersely. 'Can I come in?'

'Sure thing!' was the emphatic response. Did that sound like relief now? 'I'm too curious about this early call to turn you off, Johnny. Come into the front room.'

The front room was the parlour and Ferris led the way. It was large, gloomy, faintly musty, unused, with a picture of a young man and a young woman on the wall above the dresser. Mark Ferris and his wife. The banker's wife had died five years earlier and he had not re-married nor hired a housekeeper. There was an air of neglect everywhere, of almost total indifference to any demand for normal domesticity.

Johnny cleared his throat. 'I won't be staying long. I'd just like to ask you a couple of questions.'

Ferris laughed gruffly. He gave Johnny the impression that he was humouring him. 'I don't suppose it's to do with my visit to the sheriff? I understood that Hab would be perfectly discreet about what I told him.'

'Hab is discreet enough. But I happen to be his deputy.' Johnny felt at a loss now. He sat down on the edge of the cushioned chair indicated. 'Hab trusts me and I trust him. It's the only way two lawmen can work together.'

'Quite, quite!' Ferris ran a hand over his tousled head. 'Now, can we come to the point, Johnny?'

'Sure thing. The point is this, Mr Ferris, who else besides the sheriff and me knows about the consignment that'll be coming off the train in two days' time?'

'Why nobody, naturally. I emphasised the need for extreme care and secrecy to Hab. Why do you ask that, especially at this hour of the morning?' he added with a touch of irony.

'I got to thinking,' Johnny told him. He started to reach for his makings, changed his mind. 'I share the responsibility for the safety of that money until it's on the train going south,' he went on. 'You know about these strangers that are holed up in Mulehead Valley, I guess?'

'Yes, I do,' Ferris frowned his impatience. He perched on the edge of a large couch, tightened the robe around him. 'They seem to have created a minor scare. And I agree that Ray Glover made a mistake of judgment when — '

'The damage is done,' Johnny interrupted. 'So you're saying that nobody but you, the sheriff, and I know about the shipment? Even your tellers are in the dark?'

'Yes, they are,' was the peevish response. 'I won't take Dodd and Meeker into my confidence until the shipment is delivered. Does that satisfy you?'

Johnny nodded and rose. 'Sorry to disturb you, Mr Ferris. But you'll understand that we've got to be careful.'

'Of course,' Ferris said with sudden, bogus warmth. 'Good heavens, man, I'm only too pleased at your concern! Hab thinks highly of you, Johnny. Personally, I believe you'd have made — Well, never mind,' he finished with a patronising smile.

'So long, Mr Ferris.' Johnny preceded him to the front door and waited to be let out. 'See you, sir.'

'Thanks for coming, Johnny.'

The door shut behind him, Johnny walked along the path to the gate. He drew the gate to and replaced the small bar. A whiff of summer fragrance came from the overgrown garden. He dallied by the cottonwoods to fashion a cigarette and light it. His face wore a frown of abstraction. He shrugged and went on, but he was more thoughtful than ever as he made his way back to the hotel.

★ ★ ★

He slept until well past daybreak and awoke refreshed, despite his broken night. He washed and shaved and presented himself in the dining-room for breakfast before most of the roomers had appeared. He was on his third cup of coffee when the stout figure of Hab Beely threw a lumpy shadow across the floor. The sheriff came on in and sat down.

'Morning, Hab,' Johnny greeted with experimental cheerfulness. 'You look like you fell out of the wrong side of your tree this morning.'

'That so?' Beely grunted with a warning sneer. 'Well, you don't look like

226

a gent was on the prowl for most of the night, which you sure as hell were. What's got into you, mister? You losing your nerve?'

Johnny finished his coffee and threw a look at the street door. While shaving he had considered the advisability of telling the sheriff everything. He had been tempted to spare Hab the incident of the intruder in his room, but he knew that once he began using deceit or subterfuge he might continue doing so, with the wrong results.

'So you've been talking to Mark Ferris?'

'Not so much talking to him as him talking to me,' the sheriff snorted. 'What did you do a thing like that for? Ferris is having a good laugh to himself . . .'

'Laugh? Well, then he's got a strange sense of humour. I had a good reason for calling on him. I was curious to hear how many knew about that shipment coming in on the train. He claims he told nobody but you. He's not pleased at you taking me into your confidence.'

'He told nobody but me, of course. I could have told you that if you'd asked me. You didn't have to bother Ferris. He's a touchy character at the best of times.'

'I said I had good reason for seeing him, Hab. Mark Ferris wasn't the only one I talked to last night.'

'Oh?' Beely leaned forward. 'So what have I to do to get you to tell me?'

Johnny related how he had been roused from his sleep and everything else that had taken place subsequently. The sheriff fell back in his chair, trying to keep the slackness out of his mouth. He wiped his brow.

'You reckon it was that damned Post gent who bought the Benson place? But what did he mean by all that guff? What in hell was he driving at?'

Johnny shook his head. 'I don't know yet,' he confessed. 'But it's plain that something's in the wind, and I'm convinced it's linked to that money heading for the bank. I'm sure I know why that bunch of sidewinders hit town in the first place. They've heard about the money, Hab, one way or another. Right now they're hatching a plot to get their hands on it. Sure, Post could have killed me easy, but he had orders not to kill me. A lawman getting killed would make too big a fuss and put everybody on guard. Any scores that outfit figures on settling will be done later. *After they rob the bank or the train.*'

Hab Beely blew down his nose. He had gone a putty colour and his breathing was uneven. A waiter came to take his order but he waved him off.

He found his tongue at last. 'What — what are we going to do? What can we do without real proof?'

Any answer was precluded by the sudden arrival of a dust-covered rider from Sam Ford's Bar F ranch. He addressed Johnny without apology or preamble.

'Johnny, Sam wants you out at home *pronto.* Ginny went for a ride last night and hasn't been seen since . . . '

13

Despite Johnny's suggestion to Hab Beely that he should hold down the law office while he was gone, the sheriff insisted on saddling up and accompanying his deputy to the Bar F.

'You keep forgetting who's wearing the badge that matters in this town,' he observed acidly. 'If Sam's girl is missing I want to know why and I want to know where she is.'

Johnny made no attempt to argue at this juncture. His sole concern just then was for Ginny Ford's welfare. The cowboy messenger, Bob Crane, had not been able to embroider his terse message to any satisfactory extent. The girl had gone for a ride before sundown yesterday, and it was midnight before her father realised she was not in her room. He had checked the saddle stock and discovered that Ginny's favourite pony was missing. Ford had instigated an immediate search, covering a wide expanse of territory, but it appeared as though Ginny had vanished from the face of the earth.

Johnny's features were a grey, tight-planed mask as he pressed his bay gelding alongside the cowhand's mount. Hab Beely was slightly in the rear, setting a pace that would accommodate his mount's ability. Beely would have rounded up a band of townsmen to help him in the search, but Johnny had objected. After all, he pointed out, Sam Ford had sent for him and had not requested a posse.

'We'd better see Sam first and hear what he thinks. The way I see it, the last thing he wants is a general scare. Ginny might even be at home when we get there.'

Privately, though, Johnny did not believe they would find that Ginny had returned to the ranch and was safe and well. The crisp breeze fanning his cheeks helped clear some of the confused fancies from his mind so that he might determine a logical pattern. The pieces of the puzzle were coming together with a vengeance, and while the whole picture continued to elude him, there was a sinister element that carried its own dark cloud.

He reviewed everything of significance that had happened so far: the coming of the strangers to Stockwell, their high-handed behaviour, their open contempt for law and order. He reflected on the stranger who had been watching Ginny on her lone rides, and wondered if the key to her disappearance lay in that. The warning he had been given by the man who broke into his hotel room was another link in the chain.

'Mighty soon you're going to get news that'll upset you, kind of . . . '

This was the news he had been warned about, the disappearance of Ginny. It was not a case of her getting lost and being unable to find her way back to the ranch. It was not a case of her pony having fallen and broken a leg, leaving her stranded overnight on the range. This was a deliberate and calculated abduction.

And so his thoughts raced, frantically, out-pacing the speed of his galloping bay. The intruder had warned him not to go hog-wild when he heard. He was supposed to remain calm, to keep his wits about him. He was supposed to do only what was sensible in the context of his concern for Ginny's welfare.

His feelings were in a hopeless turmoil by the time he, Bob Crane, and Hab Beely — now straggling a quarter-mile behind — came in sight of the Bar F headquarters. He found half a dozen cowhands over by the mess-shack, horses saddled, drinking mugs of coffee to sustain them. Sam Ford emerged, weary and haggard-looking, to greet the lawmen. His eyes swept over the sheriff before he addressed his deputy.

'Glad you came, Johnny . . . Glad to see you, too, Hab. Sorry to bother you fellas, but I'm at my wits' end. We've searched everywhere we might expect to find Ginny. I've alerted my neighbours, and some of them have got their boys out searching as well. Is there a chance you know something I don't know, Johnny?'

Johnny sat for a moment in silence. Hab Beely, feeling he was obliged to take the initiative, started to suggest something but changed his mind abruptly and brought his lips together. Like Johnny, he could see a connection between the reported spying on the girl and the visit of the stranger to the deputy's hotel room. But beyond that he was baffled. 'Could I see you alone for a minute, Sam?' Johnny said.

The request surprised Sam Ford, as it did the others. But the rancher nodded and gestured to the doorway. He went into the house and Johnny followed him. In the big, shadowy living-room, Ford swung on his heel.

'Do you know what I'm beginning to think? I was going to take the boys out there myself, but something told me to 'hang fire until I saw you.'

'You're thinking of that outfit in Mulehead Valley?'

'You bet!' Ford grated. 'They're a bunch of sidewinders, and everybody knows it. They've been stalking my girl, watching every move she made. But why would they want to grab her? When I asked myself that, I decided not to do anything rash. Do you know something, Johnny?' he ended hoarsely.

'I'm glad you didn't take your boys to Mulehead. Even if Mike Wheeler and his gang did snatch Ginny, it's hardly likely she's at the old Benson place.'

'But why should they take her at all?' Ford demanded. 'Hell, you don't think — '

'No, Sam, I don't. I've got a hunch they won't hurt her — so long as things pan out the way they want them. It's really me they want to get by the short hairs.'

'But why?' the rancher cried in amazement.

'Because there'll be a hundred

thousand dollars lodged in the Stockwell bank on Thursday, that's why! They want to use me to make it easy for them.'

'But where did they get their information?'

'That's the big mystery,' Johnny said grimly. 'According to Mark Ferris, nobody was supposed to know but Ferris, Hab and me. But Wheeler and his gang must have got a tip-off. Wheeler must have a contact man somewhere, either where the money's being shipped or in Stockwell.'

'The devil you say! Who could it be? Say, you don't suppose — '

'Easy,' Johnny chided with a bleak grin. 'It's easy making guesses. We need to get evidence that'll serve as proof. But these hellions have got Ginny, and I can guess their next move . . . Will you do me a favour, Sam?'

'Anything you say,' Ford agreed promptly.

'Go out there and tell Hab you want him to accompany you. Pretend there's a section of the range you haven't searched. Just keep him out of my feet for a spell.'

'He's your boss, you know. Sometimes you act as if you're *his* boss.'

'Please, Sam!' Johnny groaned. 'I expect to get the boot when this is over anyway. But by then I won't care a hoot.'

'Tell me where you're going,' the rancher urged. 'But don't say you're going to the old Benson place on your own . . . '

'Just give me a few hours. If I'm not back here by the middle of the afternoon you can make tracks for Mulehead. Is it a deal?'

'All right,' Ford agreed reluctantly. 'It's a deal. But if anything has happened to Ginny . . . '

'Talking won't get us anywhere. Go out there and do your stuff with Hab.'

The sheriff was puzzled by the rancher's suggestion that he should ride with him and the boys in search of his daughter; his puzzlement was tempered with suspicion when his deputy declared he wanted to stay at the ranch and look around. Beely believed that Johnny had some plan of his own up his sleeve. Even so, he gave the younger man a curt nod of consent, which meant he was giving him the benefit of any doubt he had.

And so it was that five minutes later Sam Ford, with most of his crew and the sheriff, rode away from the ranch and veered into the south. Johnny waited for a while before going to saddle and facing his bay into the north-east and the direction of Mule-head Valley.

The heat was pouring down steadily when he finally reached the multi-hued rocks flanking the south side of the valley and chose one of the many notches to enter the old Benson grazing land. He was a mile below the main buildings at this point, and from there he swung east up the valley, travelling at a leisurely pace, although his nerves were strung to the limit.

He had not gone far before he sensed he was under surveillance. Sweat filmed his brow as he considered this crazy move, but it was too late now for second thoughts. He was playing what had started off as a strong hunch and he must go through with it. If the hunch proved wrong, then Sam Ford and the others might find his body when they came to look for him. Or he might vanish as effectively as Ginny Ford had vanished.

He was a quarter-mile from the old ranch-house when a scuffle in the rocks flanking the side of the trail made him whirl, right hand falling to the gun at his hip.

'Forget it, Deputy!'

There were two of them behind him, mounted, their six-shooters trained on him. They were the men called Seth and Clem. They moved in closer while he waited, hands in full view.

'That's showing sense,' Seth grunted. 'Let me have that iron.' He relieved Johnny of his Colt, then gestured to the

239

huddle of ranch buildings. 'Mike has been kind of expecting you.'

When they reached the front of the main house Mike Wheeler and Fred Post spilled out of the doorway as though they had been expecting something of this nature. The sallow-skinned man's lips bent in a twisted grin.

'Why, hello again, Johnny,' he greeted. 'Step inside.' He shot a glance at the mounted men. 'Sure he ain't got company?'

'Sure enough. He's seen the writing on the wall, I reckon.'

Johnny slid to the ground and eyed the sullen-featured Fred Post. 'You didn't leave your calling card last night, Fred. Where's Ginny?'

Wheeler chuckled. 'Ginny? I reckon that would be the pretty gal you're sweet on?'

'You know who she is, damn you,' Johnny erupted in spite of his intention to stay calm. 'You grabbed her when she was out riding. Where is she?'

'Safe enough, I guess.' Wheeler's eyes

took on the frightening wild quality of a hawk. 'You're sure Sam Ford won't make tracks for here? Because if he does . . . '

'He won't. Not yet anyway. You've made your point, mister. You snatched the girl to suit your game. You knew I'd come here and that I'd be alone. You told me to play it cool. Well, here I am, cool as you like. But if you harm a hair of Ginny's head — '

'We won't if you keep acting sensible,' Mike assured him. 'Come in and make yourself at home,' he invited, stepping inside.

Johnny was ushered into the small living-room and noticed that it had been cleaned up somewhat. There was no sign of Lute Bannon or the other two men. They were probably standing guard on Ginny, wherever she was. He didn't believe she was here at the ranch.

Mike Wheeler signalled for him to sit down on an old wire-bound chair across the table. The outlaw chief perched on the edge of the table and produced a cigar. He toyed with it in an abstracted manner.

'So far you've acted like you should, Johnny. You might call us a bunch of desperadoes and you'd be close to the mark. But money always puts a bit of iron into a man, and we're playing for high stakes.'

'A hundred thousand dollars?' Johnny said thinly. 'That's it, isn't it?'

'You've got it, pard! We aim to get that dough and we took a while to figure out the best way to go about it. Maybe you'll even appreciate that we don't hanker to spill any blood unless we have to. Understand?'

'I think so,' Johnny said from dry lips. 'The deal?'

'There's a deal, sure,' the outlaw agreed. 'You've already figured that.'

'But how did you get wind of the money coming to the bank in the first place?'

'None of your business, Johnny. Forget it.'

Johnny tried a shot in the dark. 'So

242

Mark Ferris is mixed up in it. Just like I guessed he was? He must have known well in advance and hired you boys to do his dirty work? That dynamite scare was just a trick to keep us guessing. Ferris will make sure the vault won't give you much trouble. But can you trust him, Mike? I know I wouldn't trust him as far as I could pitch him.'

'That'll do,' Wheeler cautioned, his eyes snapping in a way that told Johnny his probe had gone home. 'You can be too smart for the good of your health, mister. We've got the girl and — '

'Harm her and I'll kill you,' Johnny burst out.

Fred Post moved forward. He had been leaning against the door jamb, a cigarette trailing from the corner of his mouth. 'What the hell does it matter if the lawdog's smart?' he sneered. 'Once we get the money he can go climb a tree.'

'Shut up, Fred,' the pale-faced man warned. 'Now, Johnny, I need to know if you blabbed anything to that fat sheriff.'

'No, I didn't. But I had a job keeping Sam Ford and his boys out of here. If you fellas know what's good for you, you'll free Ginny and pull your freight out of this territory *pronto*.'

He was unprepared for Wheeler swinging a balled fist at his jaw that threw him sprawling to his knees. He raised his head, shook it. The outlaw put the bore of his gun against his temple.

'You talk too much, Johnny. All you have to do is mind your business and we'll mind ours.' He waited until Johnny had recovered and slumped on to the chair. 'Now, here's the jig, Deputy: as you already know, tomorrow night that *dinero* is going to be lodged in the town bank. We're riding in to grab it, and you're going to guarantee that nobody lifts a finger until we finish the job and clear out of town. Do you get that straight?'

Johnny nodded. He could see that

Wheeler would be totally ruthless if he was crossed or had his plans frustrated. Unless the deputy complied with his demands he really would have Ginny killed.

'What time do you aim to rob the bank?' he asked in a voice so hollow he scarcely recognized it as his own.

'That's for us to decide. You act like you do any other night. I don't care a damn how you muzzle that fat sheriff, but you'd better do it. Get me, friend?'

Johnny fingered his jaw. He ached for the opportunity to get his hands on this outlaw. But he would have to contain himself, for Ginny's sake he would have to curb his fury and keep a cool nerve.

'And that cow-rassler Ford,' Mike Wheeler persisted. 'Just you drop a word of friendly advice in his ear. Tell him to sit tight and not come near Mulehead. Tell him he needn't try finding his girl because he won't find her.'

'When will he find her?' Johnny demanded bitterly.

'Soon enough. You keep your side of the bargain and we'll keep ours. Give him his gun, Seth. See he leaves the valley. The rest is up to you, Mr Carver. If you don't do as you're told you'll never see the Ford girl alive again. Now . . . get the hell out of here.'

As a precaution before handing him his weapon, Seth punched the shells out of the chambers. Johnny took the Colt, holstered it. He went out to the sunshine, brow layered with cold sweat. He mounted the bay and rode east, towards the main exit. When he had travelled a hundred yards or so heard two riders following him at a distance. He left the valley without a backward glance and picked up the main trail to Stockwell.

After a mile or so he swung southerly and then bent to the west. He arrived at Bar F headquarters as the bunch of cowhands led by Sam Ford and the sheriff rode in from their search.

Hab Beely's face was like thunder as he dropped from his saddle and made a beeline towards him. His anger merely fuelled Johnny's own fury and frustration.

'All right, boy,' the lawman flashed. 'This has gone just about as far as it'll stretch. If you don't spell everything out so that even a dunce like me can understand you can peel that badge off right now.'

'No call to shout at me, Hab. We'll talk inside with Sam, if that suits you . . . Can we go inside, Sam?'

They sat in the coolness of the big living-room and Johnny related everything that happened, leaving out no detail. When it was brought home to him that his daughter really was in the hands of the Mulehead Valley gang, Sam Ford swore long and luridly. Then he grabbed his hat and ducked for the door. Johnny yelled after him.

'Come back, damn it! Now, you'd better listen, Sam,' he snarled when the cowman paused. 'I'll lock you in irons if I have to so you'll not put Ginny's life at risk. We need to keep our heads. I'm sure Ginny's safe for the minute. We know they're after that money, and that they're using Ginny to get their hands on it. And pay heed to this, Hab,' he added to the bleak-eyed sheriff, 'Mark Ferris is in cahoots with them. I found that out as well.'

Hab Beely stared as though his deputy had finally lost his senses. Sam Ford went into another bout of swearing.

'I'll wring the bastard renegade's neck!' he exploded.

'Later, maybe. It was as big a shock to me as it is to you. But there had to be a leak somewhere. You knew that, Hab, didn't you?'

Beely nodded heavily, yielding to the younger man's logic. He followed Sam Ford out to the porch where the foreman and several cowhands were still hanging around in the yard. There, he swung on Johnny, eyes fiery with purpose.

'If you think I'm going to lie down under this, you're wrong, boy. No matter what kind of deal they made with you.'

'Never said we were going to lie down. But you've got to play these fellas at their own game, Hab.'

'How?' Sam Ford demanded, unconvinced.

'We'll pretend to go along with their scheme, Sam. We've got another day left and we'll have to make use of it to find out where they've got Ginny.'

14

Where to look for Ginny?

Johnny knew this end of the range as well as anyone else. He proposed searching the woods, the line houses used by the ranchers — especially those that had fallen into disuse during the past year or so. To each of his suggestions Sam Ford shook his head wearily. He had explored this angle as well and had ordered every cabin and shack on his land to be investigated. His neighbours, alerted to Ginny's disappearance, had conducted similar searches. He had been forced to the conclusion that Ginny was a prisoner in Mulehead Valley.

'I'll take my boys there and flush that damned bunch out,' he decided. 'If they want a fight they can have one.'

'Not so fast, Sam,' Johnny objected. 'You'd say these hellions would keep

Ginny where we'd be least likely to suspect, wouldn't you?'

'Mulehead Valley,' Ford said emphatically. 'Can you think of anywhere else?'

'Maybe.' Johnny drew the sheriff aside and spoke hurriedly to him. Hab Beely's face creased in disbelief before his jaw dropped.

'Blazes, I never thought of that! Let's go then.'

The two lawmen went to saddle and a puzzled Sam Ford hastened to grip the gelding's reins.

'What's the big idea? If you're going to Mulehead, me and the boys are going along.'

'Never said Mulehead,' Johnny told him. 'We're headed for town, Sam. I'm playing a hunch that might pay off. Stay where you are until you hear from us. Hold your boys in readiness and let one of them come to town with Hab and me.'

'You can take Bob Crane. But how do you expect to find Ginny in town?'

251

'Like I said, I've got a hunch. And remember, don't go near Mulehead until you get the word.'

'I hope you know what you're doing, Sheriff.'

'Me?' Beely growled. 'I'm just the errand boy here. But I think I know what's on his mind, Sam, and if he's wrong he's going to have to crawl from here to away over yonder.'

He and Johnny travelled for a while in silence, each busy with his own thoughts. Bob Crane was content to ride out on their left flank, his sun-darkened face inscrutable. He was one of Sam Ford's most trusted hands.

Excitement was high in Johnny at this stage; he had no doubt that Mark Ferris was mixed up with the strangers. Ferris would have known for quite a while about the consignment of money arriving in Stockwell. Somehow or other he had got in touch with Mike Wheeler to help him with his scheme. The outlaws would be blamed for the theft and later, when the dust settled,

Ferris could pull out with the lion's share. No one in town would suspect an upright, straitlaced character like Mark Ferris of being a thief.

The trouble was, Johnny reflected, he had alerted the outlaw leader to his suspicions concerning the bank manager. Therefore, Wheeler might have warned Ferris to be on guard. Even so, a man with the kind of nerve needed to plot such a robbery would have the nerve to try and brazen it out.

They reached Stockwell at length and headed straight for the law office. Johnny realised that some of the Mulehead Valley bunch might be watching his movements. Mike Wheeler would have detailed a man to keep him under surveillance. With this in mind, he asked Bob Crane to go through the back alleys and find a position on the outskirts of town where he could observe the western trail without being seen by an oncoming rider.

'Stay there for ten minutes or so, Bob, then come back here.'

'Sure thing, Johnny.'

Johnny followed Hab Beely into the office side, but Beely swept to the street door again in a restless fashion. 'Maybe we ought to search Mark's house first off,' he suggested. 'And you'd better be sure you've got this right, boy. If Ferris happens to be innocent you'll go out of this burg on a rail.'

Johnny smiled bleakly. 'I've already considered the risk, Hab. But I don't care as long as Ginny is found safe. No, I don't think Ferris would hide an abducted girl in his own house. She'll be somewhere else so that he can keep his hands clean if she's found before they're ready to release her.'

Beely slammed a fist into a cupped palm. 'If he's really in with those hellions he's a right bastard, mister.'

Johnny just nodded. They smoked and let the time drag. On the street the sun burned down relentlessly. At last they heard a horse outside, and soon Bob Crane ducked in from the sunlight.

'Nobody on our back-trail for sure,

Sheriff,' he announced.

'Good,' Johnny grunted. 'Here's what I suggest, Hab: you stroll along Lincoln Avenue and plant yourself near enough to the front of the banker's house. I'll take Bob along the alley and search the outhouses. It's a cinch somebody will be on guard where they're holding Ginny.'

The sheriff resented the subsidiary role being forced on him, but he had decided to go along with his young deputy, having more faith in him than he would admit. In any case, he believed Johnny might be on the right track.

'This is your show,' he said with the merest trace of warning in his tone. 'Let's give it a whirl.'

The three men walked to the Lincoln Avenue — Main Street intersection together. They did their best to appear casual about what they were doing, although it would in no ways fool a spy from Mulehead Valley. Johnny took a look into the tree-lined avenue.

'It's all yours, Hab. We'll back-track a piece and go into the first alley.'

The sheriff did not enter Lincoln Avenue at once. Instead, he hurried on easterly for three blocks, until he was on a level with the front window of the National Bank. It was a simple enough matter to peer through the window without arousing interest in himself. He saw the manager talking with one of his tellers. The banker and the teller were bent over a ledger. What had gone wrong with someone supposedly as rigidly puritanical as Mark Ferris?

Hab exchanged greetings with several passers-by before he withdrew. His lips firmed when he considered how Ferris had probably been fooling — and fleecing — his customers all these years. Johnny could be wrong, though. Perhaps he was allowing his concern for the welfare of Ginny Ford to warp his thinking. But no, he must be right.

Hab swung away towards Lincoln Avenue.

★　★　★

Johnny and Bob Crane trod several alleys and open lots to gain the alleyway running along the rear of Lincoln. Directly opposite Mark Ferris' back door was a substantial outhouse which the banker used for storage purposes. They stopped short of the building and studied the area before Johnny approached the single narrow doorway. He noticed that the door had a hasp for a padlock, without a padlock being in place. Still, there could be a bolt on the inside, and he prayed that this wild hunch of his would pay off.

He listened for a few seconds, but heard nothing. Then, winking at the watchful Bob Crane who was standing at the ready, hand on gun butt, Johnny brought his own gun to hand and rapped with his knuckles, then put his ear to the rough timber. Nothing. He swallowed hard and cuffed moisture from his brow. His heart skipped a beat when he heard a scuffle on the other side of the door. Someone spoke querulously.

'Who's there?'

'Me — Ferris.'

He stepped back as a bolt was drawn. The door swung open and he glimpsed two things at once — the lean, wolfish face of Lute Bannon and the six-shooter Bannon poked forward menacingly.

Had Bannon triggered immediately it would have been all over for Johnny Carver. But the outlaw's first impulse was to slam the door in the deputy's face. It was the vital indecision and fractional delay that proved the lanky man's downfall. Johnny gave the door a violent heave that threw Bannon off balance. Then, as the outlaw steadied himself to shoot, Johnny surged in on him, gun barrel rising and coming down in a short, vicious chop. Lute Bannon grunted and slithered to the earthen floor.

Colt levelled, Johnny crossed a small room that was cluttered with old furniture to gain the doorway of another room at the rear. He charged through, prepared to drill anyone who tried to impede him. He came up short, a strangled oath shivering from his lips, at sight of Ginny Ford, bound and gagged, in a rickety straight-backed chair.

Fear had shone in the wide eyes that stared at him, but now that fear turned to relief. Ginny began to cry, her sobs smothered by the bandanna tied fast around her mouth.

'It's all right, honey. I'll soon have you out of this . . . '

He worked feverishly to release her. Bob Crane had dashed into the building behind him. The cowhand took a look at the unconscious Lute Bannon, then joined the deputy in the ante-room. By then Ginny was in Johnny's arms, talking and sobbing in the one breath, trying to describe how they had waylaid her and made her captive.

'You can tell me later,' he panted,

leading her to the outer door. 'Bob, rope that gent up good and leave him where he is for the time being. Then hunt up Hab and tell him to wait for me in the office.'

He took the girl along the back alleys until they arrived at the hotel. They went up the back staircase to the catwalk. The escape door was unlocked and he pushed it inwards. A few moments later he gained his own room. So far, he was pretty sure they had not been observed.

'This is your room, Johnny! But I don't want to stay here.' She was on the verge of panic. 'I want to go home. Dad will be at his wits' end with worry, and — '

'Listen, honey, I want you to stay here for a short time. I'll be back soon enough. I'll see the clerk downstairs and get him to fetch you anything you need. You'll do what I ask, Ginny? I want you under cover until we get the drop on the rest of this outfit.'

She shuddered and held him tightly

for a moment. He kissed her brow and released himself.

'Be careful, Johnny, won't you? And hurry back . . . '

'Don't worry. Just do as I say and everything will turn out fine.'

He hurried from the room and closed the door behind him. Downstairs, he held a whispered conversation with the clerk. The man's jaw sagged in surprise, but he finally understood and nodded vigorously.

'Leave everything to me, Johnny. Nobody's going to know where Miss Ford's at. I'll watch everything until you get back.'

Hab Beely had joined Bob Crane in the law office by the time he arrived there. Beely's face had a dark hue that betrayed the unusual excitement he felt.

'So your hunch was right!' he exulted. 'Bannon's roped up good in the outhouse, Bob says. But this renegade Ferris — '

'We'll deal with him *pronto* . . . Bob, here's another chore for you: get along to the bank and tell Mark Ferris the sheriff wants to see him for a minute. Don't say anything else, no matter what he asks.'

'I get your drift.'

The cowhand had a grim smile at his lips as he ducked out to the sunshine. He was pleased at being chosen for this important role in the smashing of the Mulehead Valley gang.

'We've got Ferris cold, Hab, and he can't deny it. The minute he steps through that door we poke a gun in his belly and lock him up in a cage.'

'Bastard!' the sheriff snarled, still shocked to the core by the enormity of the bank manager's treachery. 'He must have been in a bad way to go to such lengths. Well, I'm just dying to see his face when he gets here.'

Hab saw the banker's face a short time later. Mark Ferris was frowning as he entered from the street. He halted abruptly when the expressions on the features of the two lawmen registered. Then something told him he was walking into a trap. He emitted a strangled oath, whirled, and charged for the street. Bob Crane was already there and the cowhand grappled with him and heaved him back to the office.

'Too late for running, you skunk. You should have made tracks long ago.'

★　★　★

A little while afterwards, Johnny and Bob Crane rode out of town together. In the meantime, the bank manager had been locked up and been joined by Lute Bannon brought from Ferris' outhouse. A lot had been accomplished, Johnny reflected as he and Ford's rider galloped along the trail to the Bar F headquarters, but a lot more remained to be done before they could call it a day.

Johnny's chief worry now was that Mike Wheeler might somehow hear what had taken place. Wheeler had trusted Lute Bannon to stand guard on Ginny Ford, but the outlaw boss might have detailed someone to back up Bannon. Johnny and his companion kept a sharp look-out as they travelled, and when they were within a mile of Bar F, Sam Ford and his foreman rode out to meet them. Johnny lost no time in assuring the rancher that his daughter was safe, but warned him that there was more to be done before they could wipe the slate clean.

'Ferris must have been in a mighty bad way to pull such a trick,' he observed grimly.

'Why don't we ride into town and string him up?' one of the Bar F cowboys growled. 'It's what he deserves.'

'He'll get what he deserves,' Johnny said sternly. 'I'm riding for Mulehead,' he told the rancher. 'I'm hoping they believe everything is going to plan so that we can catch them flatfooted. I could use you and your boys now, Sam.'

'Then let's go, by heck! Phil, you cut back and get the rest of the men. Tell them to tag along with Johnny, Hack and me.'

Soon the little band was heading into the north-east. The sun was bright overhead and the rangeland shimmered in the haze. Johnny chose the entrance to the valley he thought would afford the best chance of surprise. He broke through at length with fifteen battle-hungry cowmen in his wake. They would ride straight to the old ranch-house and call on Mike Wheeler and his men to surrender.

'If they want a fight we'll oblige, with bells on,' he vowed.

They were a scant hundred yards from the ramshackle building when two of the outlaws leaped through the front door of the house and hit the yard. Three others followed rapidly. It was Mike Wheeler who opened the ball. Wheeler, realising that something had gone badly wrong with his plans, pumped off a rifle bullet. Then he bounded to the corner of the house, intent on reaching the corral and grabbing a horse. Sam Ford and the others closed in.

'Hold it, Wheeler!' Johnny yelled. 'The rest of you as well . . . '

A ragged volley of gunfire answered him. The outlaws knew what lay in store for them if they were captured, and while there was no chance of reaching their horses they were determined to make a fight of it. Six-shooters and rifles banged spitefully and bullets sliced hither and yonder. The Mulehead Valley gang scattered to whatever cover was available — the water barrel at the corner of the house, the rock surround of the yard pump, the trees and brush screenings.

'Let's take them, boys!'

Sam Ford and his crew needed no second bidding; they fanned out in a loose circle, holding their fire until they were facing the ranch-house. Then they tightened the circle, at the same time raking the area with volley after volley of rifle and six-gun fire.

Johnny spotted a man skirting a

clump of brush and making a wild break back to the rickety front porch. He aimed without compunction, triggered to the hard rhythm of his Colt bucking against the palm of his hand. The man's stride faltered, became a tangle of legs that had turned to pieces of string. Another outlaw dashed after his comrade and was torn around in a bloody bundle. The circle closed tighter still.

Two more outlaws were cut down as they tried to reach the corral and their horses. And in the middle of the clamour Mike Wheeler, the leader of the bunch, shrilled an acknowledgement of defeat.

'Hold your fire . . . Don't shoot, damn you!'

'Damn *you*,' Johnny flung at him. 'All right then. Stand up and elevate. And tell your pard there to do the same.'

The pale-faced man emerged slowly from the direction of the barn, arms held high. He kept up a disjointed garble that made Johnny's stomach turn.

'It wasn't me who planned it, Deputy, it was Ferris at the bank. He contacted a gent who knew me and we met secretly in Darton's back room. He planned the whole thing, told us to grab the girl so you'd stand off and let us get the money. Your girl's all right, Carver.'

'We know where she is,' Sam Ford interjected bitterly. 'We know where Ferris is, too — in the hoosegow. We tumbled to his game and — Hey, catch him, boys!'

Mike Wheeler had taken off at a wild run and was bolting for the corner of the main building. Johnny dropped to one knee and aiming carefully, he triggered. Mike Wheeler appeared to leap into the air before going into a crazy somersault. He crashed down and lay, writhing and screaming, grasping his shattered left leg.

Ford's men completed their pincer manoeuvre while Johnny punched spent shells from his gun and reloaded.

'That's the roost stripped, Sam,' he

declared. 'Bring those birds to town, will you?'

'Where you heading?' Ford wanted to know.

'Town,' Johnny explained with a tight grin. 'But I want to travel light. I promised Ginny I wouldn't be long. I'll bring her straight home.'

He was soon in the saddle and riding hard to pick up the Stockwell trail. When the dust had settled he would call Ray Glover again and keep a gun pointed at the land agent's nose until he clinched the deal for this valley.

In some perverse fashion he had grown fond of Mulehead and felt that, having helped purge it, he would like to see cattle grazing across yonder, and perhaps have a few hogs and chickens. But of course he would have to get Ginny's approval and make certain she would enjoy being a cowman's wife as well as a cowman's daughter.

Matt Matthews had carved his ranch out of the wild Wyoming frontier. But he had his troubles. The big blow of '86 was catastrophic, with dead beeves littering the plains, and the oncoming winter presaged worse. On top of this, a gang of desperadoes had moved into the Snake River valley, killing, raping and rustling. All Matt can do is to take on the killers single-handed. But will he escape the hail of lead?

RODEO RENEGADE

Ty Kirwan

When English couple Rufus and Nancy Medford inherit a ranch in New Mexico, they find the majority of their neighbours are hostile to strangers. Befriended by only one rancher, and plagued by rustlers, the thought of returning to England is tempting, but needing to prove himself, Rufus is coached as a fighter by a circus sharp shooter, the mysterious Ghost of the Cimarron. But will this be enough to overcome the frightening odds against him?

BRAZOS STATION

Clayton Nash

Caleb Brett liked his job as deputy sheriff and being betrothed to the sheriff's daughter, Rose. What he didn't like was the thought of the sheriff moving in with them once they were married. But capturing the infamous outlaw Gil Bannerman offered a way out because there was plenty of reward money. Then came Brett's big mistake — he lost Bannerman and was framed. Now everything he treasured was lost. Did he have a chance in hell of fighting his way back?

THE WIND WAGON

Troy Howard

Sheriff Al Corning was as tough as they came and with his four seasoned deputies he kept the peace in Laramie — at least until the squatters came. To fend off starvation, the settlers took some cattle off the cowmen, including Jonas Lefler. A hard, unforgiving man, Lefler retaliated with lynchings. Things got worse when one of the squatters revealed he was a former Texas lawman — and no mean shooter. Could Sheriff Corning prevent further bloodshed?